Dear **BIG Human-Bean!**

Did you KNOW?

Ms K.J. Kaschula has created some
BRAVE-Activities
right here on her website just for your
Super-Dooper-A-MAZE-ZING
little human-beans!

Search and find them at:
www.kjkaschula.com

This Brave Kids Book
is Gifted to:

_____

Brave Kids

Short Stories to Inspire
Our Future World-Changers

Volume 2

K. J. Kaschula

Featuring: Rose Aehle, Dr. Shelley Astrof, Indya J. Clark, Kelly Daugherty, Susan Ernst, Carrie Freshour, Dr. George Garcia, Terri Hawke, MJ Luna, Dr. Heidi MacAlpine, Dr. Charleen M. Michel, Samara Ena Minichiello, Cedric Nwafor, Dr. Pamela J. Pine, Eileen Poniński, Janice Pratt, N.S. Shakti, Meredith Speir, TJ STAR, Timothy Stuetz, Susan Thompson, Lorie Weed, Atlantis Wolf

Contents

Foreword

To feast my eyes and soul upon this magnificent book has been a gift bigger than I imagined.

Can it get any better? That's what I thought after we published the first Brave Kids collaboration. That first book was the beginning of a big vision and dream, and kicked off a cascade of kids book awesomeness.

I've watched the brilliant mind of lead author K.J. Kaschula as she made her dream a reality and brought together her co-authors with a kind, gentle, and child-like spirit, but also with a dedicated mission to bring the most magnificent stories to life. Every time we gather together for these projects, something magical and profound happens—a big love energy grows and expands. Our team of authors are the magicians, manifestors, dreamers, healers, and brilliant wordsmiths, who truly and deeply care about our world and its future. What an honor to be here with all of them.

You're about to step into an adventure unlike any other.

The authors who said yes to this project stepped in and showed up with their full hearts, beginner's minds, and pure passion. You'll feel it on every single page, in every line, in every thoughtful illustration, and in every important message.

Both our returning authors and our new ones came together from all over the globe with a special energy and mission—to inspire our future world-changers. Allow this magic and intention to delight, transport, and transform you.

It's time to board this ship. You're in the safest of hands—your captain and 23 expert crew-people have walked where you're about to walk, and will guide your journey with the utmost awareness, respect, and honor. It's with ginormous gratitude that I write this foreword, and bring the following brave words into the world!

Laura Di Franco,
CEO of Brave Healer Productions and
Brave Kids Books

Introduction

All aboard, the HMS Explorer!

Laydays and *gentlemans.*

Bois and *gals.*

We—

yes, you and I,

are 'bout to begin our *voi-age* into uncharted waters filled *wit* all kids. . .

. . . I mean kinds of magical, yes mystical brave talking creatures, *'hoo* live in the fantastical—yet very *realistic'al* stories, (which I may like to add), your kid (or inner-kid's) imagination can only dream 'bout!

I am the captain of this ship—a Ms. K.J. Kaschula, and I can tell you that I have seen and, of course, read some wonderful things, but nothing as magical as what is going to transpire when you read or hear or even listen to the tales that follow within these uncharted waters.

There are dragons and mermaids and talking monkeys!

And cats of plenty and dogs of one-of-a-kind!

O', and a mango-loving crocodile and a honeybee *'hoo* bumped into a beary bear.

There are gardens, and forests, and jungles to explore!

But. . .

   . . . better beware for where there is adventure, there could also be dangerous danger! Danger of loss, danger of stage fright, danger in learning humongous words, and wonderful, outrageous danger in metamorphosis, or better known to you as:

**topsy-turvy, sometimes terrifying,
but also terrific transformation!**

Now. . .

. . .I knows *wot* you are *tinking*. . .

. . .And I can *as-sir* you that there will be many, many stops along the way for you to take care of business, like go to school or work, sleep or even eat—no worries 'bout that!

You can read or listen, or listen and read to one of four-and-twenty stories at night, and then read or listen, or listen and read to another story some other day—whatever and whenever you feel like it! However, if you are feeling really brave and up for a challenge, then you can read the whole lot in one go! It is entirely up to you!

Now along your journey, dear passenger, you will be presented with special author-like teachers offering special training and wisdom to any who dare enter their story-classroom with bright and *sparkly* eyes ready to take on the grand adventure of life and the living of it! So, as your Captain K.J. Kaschula, I *advises* you to take up the most com-fort-able chair you can find and bring your *best'est* friend—be it a teddy bear, a white rabbit, or the *King* of dogs and sits-back and relax as you read or listen to a *Brave Kids* short story from these special author-like-teachers.

There is one more thing, though. . .

It has to do with *someting* very important for you to knows. . .

O' yes, now I *remembers*. . .

We will be traveling through uncharted waters, yes—but, some waters have already been charted, that is to say, that some stories which are 'bout to unfold have already been told within the first *voi-age* or volume of the *Brave Kids* books.

If you would like to read up or listen to those first adventures and connect with the characters and their stories, then you most certainly can. Head over to Amazon or your local bookstore and place your ticket order for the *Brave Kids voi-age* 1 adventure.

And now, without further ado,

Brave Kids, voi-age—volume 2!

K.J. Kaschula

Capitan of the HMS Explorer

The following chapter
and the short stories that follow
require great imagination.

If you would like to know more
about Child White Dragon and her sisters,
you can jump to the end of this *Brave Kids, Volume 2* book
and read their introductions.

Chapter 1

Child White Dragon
By K.J. Kaschula

Part 1: Meditation

Open your eyes,
whispered the Great Tree Spirit.

"My eyes are open."
Then close them, dear Child,
for only when your eyes are closed will you truly be able to see.

*

Upon *a* floating rock
sat the one named Child.

Upon *the* floating rock
sat Child deeply beguiled.

Upon *this* floating rock
sat Child, the white dragon, in mindful contemplation.

Its dragon legs folded into one another,
and its dragon palms folded upon one another.

Its dragon eyes closed upon the world of the floating rocks,
and its dragon spirit opened up to the beyond. . .

Upon the floating rocks grew seedlings of the Great Tree Spirit. Their leaves shimmered in gold as they played with the new rays of the dawn light and glimmered in silver as they passed the rays over to the dusk light. At the base of the seedlings' trunks, on top of their golden glowing, growing roots, slept many a stone dragon.

Some of these dragons who slept upon the floating rocks under the seedlings of the Great Tree Spirit had what looked like pieces of stone missing from their stone splendor. In its place where the stone should have been, glowed moving light. Some lights glowed blue, some glowed red, some green, some yellow, and some in colors never before seen by a human eye.

Floating rocks of all shapes and sizes were scattered in what was called the In-Between.

It was called the In-Between because alongside it, on either side, sat two giants who towered over Child White Dragon. These giants were part of a special kind of family tree, a family known to you, dear reader or dear listener of this story, as a Universe.

Sister Universe, one was called.

And Brother Universe, the other was called.

The floating rocks, it was said by the Great Tree Spirit who spoke to Child White Dragon in thought, were once part of a planet that strayed too close to the edge of a universe.

Neither Sister Universe nor Brother Universe would ever tell Child White Dragon from which universe it came, only that when the planet tried to enter the In-Between, it was destroyed. From its destruction came the floating rocks and the birth of the dragon spirits who would now act as the guardians and gatekeepers to the In-Between, protecting it from any rogue planets and all the chaos it might bring.

Upon *one* floating rock within the In-Between

sat the one named Child White Dragon.

Deep in thought.

Deep in contemplation.

Deep in meditation.

Its dragon's mind extended to the far reaches of space, of time, of dimensions, and of thought.

The world of the In-Between, however, only extended as far as the very edge of Sister Universe and as far as the very edge of Brother Universe. Beyond this edge, which acted as a barrier separating the floating rocks from each universe, was and still is their kingdom—it is a kingdom which, in turn, is a universe filled with all kinds of galaxies and celestial beings.

While Child White Dragon sat in thought, in contemplation, and in meditation, Sister Universe and Brother Universe watched. . .

"What do you SEE, dear Child?"

whispered Sister Universe,
who watched from Sunrise East,
to Child White Dragon
who sat upon the floating rock.

"And, what do you HEAR, dear Child?"

whispered Brother Universe,
who watched from Sunset West,
to Child White Dragon
who sat under a seedling
of the Great Tree Spirit.

"I see a human child asleep in their bed with a brave book tucked under its pillow near its head, dreaming of the In-Between," answered Child White Dragon. "I hear the snores of a cheetah of light who saved the night.

"I see a young girl upon the pavement floor. Her heart is sad for she is mad, but a gift of a feather came from the crying weather. This brought her mother and her back together.

"I hear a boy shout ouch! And upon one leg dance about. Inside his pocket was a school letter that did not make him feel any better. Then a monkey appeared who helped him persevere."

The images and the sounds came clearly to the mind of Child White Dragon. The moving pictures raced to the center stage of the dragon's mind, and the sounds that followed bounced from thought to image to the all-seeing eye.

"What do you SMELL, dear Child?"

whispered Sister Universe
keen to know more.

"And what do you TASTE, dear Child?"

whispered Brother Universe
keen to know more too.

"I smell spring daffodils as they bloom towards the sky and see an earth spirit help them as they droop towards the ground to die."

"I taste the winter nuts Mother Squirrel has stored for her family of kits, but inside her nest, I see sibling conflicts."

The sweet spring smells of daffodils drifted in from the stage wings of the mind, and a nutty taste sprang to life from a trap door that opened up to reveal its hidden magic.

And, dear Child,
whispered the Great Tree Spirit
who watched and listened,
to the conversations of the three,

What do you FEEL?

"I feel a gentle breeze as it dances across the Kesari flowers. I see it comb through a lion cub's mane and a sheep's woolly wool for what seems like hours upon hours."

"I feel—" answered Child White Dragon, "the spirits of the many. And these spirits are just a few of what is known as the plenty."

Part 2: Contemplation

Child White Dragon opened its eyes.

There were tasks to be done in the In-Between, and only Child White Dragon, being of a dragon spirit, could perform this routine, for the changing winds were due to arrive, and its coming made Child White Dragon feel very alive.

There were tasks to be done in the In-Between, tasks of greeting, and tasks of flight.

Tasks of meeting and seeing, and if necessary, defeating with great might any who would delight in colliding a universe with another, be it a sister with its brother.

There were tasks to be done in the In-Between for *if* a universe should cross the In-Between, then the serene scene will become one where a dragon guardian and a dragon gatekeeper would have to intervene.

Child White Dragon
who sat upon a floating rock
stretched up long and tall.

Child White Dragon
who sat under a seedling of the Great Tree Spirit
stretched up high and began to fly.

From floating rock. . . .
. . . . .to floating rock. . . . .
. . . .to floating rock it flew.

Greeting. . . .
. . . . .each stone dragon. . . . .
. . . .it knew.

Many stone dragons who were once Child-like dragons slept peacefully upon their chosen rocks under the protection of the seedlings who watched over their stone slumber.

Each came before Child White Dragon, and each had turned into stone when it came time for their dragon spirit to venture forth upon their next quest.

Child White Dragon knew not the quest the stone-dragons'-spirits were on while they slumbered as stone, only that the quest taken had resulted in the separation of a dragon spirit into the many, many sparks of light.

Each spark, it was said by the Great Tree Spirit, was a light of the dragon's spirit.

Each light, it was said by the Great Tree Spirit, was tasked with a specific task.

And each task, it was said by the Great Tree Spirit, was a life lived within a universe.

Only when *one* life's task was completed would the *one* spark of the dragon's light return to its stone dragon.

When all the dragon's sparks had returned, the dragon's spirit would rise up from its stone dragon slumber in full glory to join the Great Tree Spirit and begin another, new life-quest which was unknown to all who came before and all who would come after.

As Child White Dragon flew in the In-Between the Great Tree Spirit whispered to its dragon heart,

> Tell me, dear Child,
> what do you KNOW?

It was known to Child White Dragon that Sister Universe and Brother Universe were just two of many universes that existed in the In-Between. That within their vast and incomprehensible bodies, which housed the galaxies and the celestial beings called stars and planets, creatures of various shapes and sizes were all living the spark of a life somewhere within their universe-like bodies.

It was known to Child White Dragon that each creature, animal and plant, rock and mountain, raindrop and river were gifted with a spark of a soul who was once part of a greater being. Some were once sparks of the now stone dragons who slept upon the floating rocks. Some were once sparks of other, unnamed, unknown universal guardians.

It was known that each spark's journey was an important dragon stone puzzle piece and that a dragon's spirit could not dance with the Great Tree Spirit unless all dragon stone puzzle pieces were returned to the sleeping stone dragon.

"I know," answered Child White Dragon as it flew, "that each spark of light, be they dragon or not, all ride upon the ocean waves of life's journey.

"Sometimes each wave rises like the sun,
reaching for the clear oceans of light blue.

"Sometimes each wave sets like the moon
surrendering to murky oceans of dark blue.

"Sometimes the clear oceans of light blue last for a second; sometimes they can last a lifetime.

"Sometimes the oceans of dark blue can stretch on forever, and sometimes they can stretch on for just a moment."

Part 3: Observation

Child White Dragon glided from side to side.

From the edge of Sister Universe to the edge of Brother Universe.

Sparks of dragon light glittered deep within each universe. These sparks seemed to dance and sing, rise up and fall. They blinked and twinkled. They shone brightly, some dimmed slightly. They came at times together. They drifted at times alone.

One spark which Child White Dragon observed was a child asleep in their bed. One spark a young girl upon the pavement floor. One spark a young boy dancing on one leg. One spark a spring daffodil saying goodnight as it drooped its head. Sparks of one family of kits overcoming their sibling conflicts. And a spark of the eastern wind who chose to dance with a lion, a flock of sheep, and the Kesari plants.

Each spark of light within Sister Universe and within Brother Universe was mesmerizing to behold. They were always moving. Always dancing upon their own universe's stage. And oh, what a beautiful stage it was, and so vast that they, the sparks of light could not even understand or conceive of its universal vastness, of its being, of its core, of its heartbeat, of its life within Sister Universe, and of its life within Brother Universe.

It's the dance of life.
Sister Universe called it,
who watched from Sunrise East.

It's the dance of living.
Brother Universe called it
who watched from Sunset West.

"It's the dance of being alive."
Child White Dragon called it
who watched from the In-Between.

"Oh, how I long to dance like a spark of light within a universe. But, I am afraid of the stone dragon's slumber and the unknown beyond," Child White Dragon whispered aloud as it watched as the many different color sparks would lift themselves up, twirl around, jump, then glide until they suddenly stopped.

Some sparks of light would fall, then become silent. Learn, then grow brighter.

Other sparks of light would dim. Lower. Slower. Softer in their movements, softer in their dance.

One spark, which Child White Dragon observed. . .

. . . one which had danced a full life, one which had lived a full dance, floated up and up and up, then rushed towards something— rushing towards someone. Past the celestial planets it flew, past the celestial stars it soared, past each galaxy-swirling-print, into the darkness, into the light, towards the edge, towards the very barrier separating a universe from the In-Between.

The spark of light of one who had returned home then landed upon a stone dragon.

Each spark that had returned and which had danced upon the ocean waves of life, of living, of being alive within a universal being, then began to vibrate and hum together.

The leaves of the seedling tree who watched over this stone dragon applauded the dragon's final spark's arrival. Its golden glowing roots grew further upon the stone dragon, greeting it, eager to hear the spark's story, eager to see its adventure beyond the In-Between through its all-seeing roots. The celebration of the many now became the celebration of the one dragon spirit.

The dragon stone puzzle now whole.

The dragon stone puzzle now one.

The dragon stone puzzle now none.

The spirit of this stone dragon, upon the floating rock, under the seedling Great Tree Spirit, arose from its stone slumber in pure brilliant blue light.

The blue dragon spirit looked at Child White Dragon then whispered to its heart,

Don't be afraid, dear Child.

I stood once where you stand now
upon the air separating Sister Universe and Brother Universe,
and I, too, feared the unknown.

But not knowing is the greatest adventure you could ever contemplate.

It is only when you cross the barrier
of what is known into what is unknown
that you will truly live the contemplated adventure.

The blue dragon spirit then curled inward, spiraling its magnificent body towards its center, and in an instant, the dragon spirit's center, now a brilliant ball of all different colored sparks of light, gave one last twinkle and disappeared into a new ether, into a new space, a new time, a new dance.

Into a new great adventure quest.

Part 4: Transformation

Child White Dragon felt its own sparks of light, eager to dance and ride upon their own ocean waves of life's journey.

The sparks of Child White Dragon had observed the before and had just seen the after. They were ready to rise with the moon and set with the sun.

The winds of change grew and blew in full force, pushing Child White Dragon closer to the edge of a universe, to the edge of the barrier, to the edge of the In-Between.

The stone from which the blue dragon spirit had just emerged began to crack and crumble, giving life to New Child, a new stone dragon spirit, a new guardian of the In-Between.

It is time, dear Child,

whispered the Great Tree Spirit
to Child White Dragon,
the once guardian and gatekeeper of the In-Between.

Child White Dragon took a deep breath as the sparks of light within pulled forward.

Its dragon legs folded into one another,

and its dragon palms folded upon one another.

Its dragon eyes closed upon the world of the floating rocks,

and its dragon spirit opened up to the beyond. . .

As Child White Dragon pushed headfirst forward into the unknown, sparks of every color of light flew forth in every direction.

Through space.

Through time.

Through dimension.

Through Sister Universe.

Through Brother Universe.

Through to one named New Child
who sat upon a floating rock.

It's time,
whispered the Great Tree Spirit
to open your eyes.

RETURNING STORIES

Dear passengers,

Have you heard of Chann's talking monkey? Or Sundance, the brave buckskin stallion colt? Amaleigha, a third-grade student who tamed a bully, or Daniel, who caught his negative thoughts before they ruined his day? How 'bout Caroline, who dealt with the dreaded D-word, or Shep, who conquered monkey brain?

If you have, then I *welcomes* you back upon this *voi-age*. You are in for a real treat as these characters chose to continue their brave journey with us.

If you have not, then guess *wot*?

The characters in the following story adventures have another delightful story to tell you within their first *voi-age* of *Brave Kids,* volume 1.

Chapter 2

Jasmine Saves the Day!
Trusting Your Instincts
By Susan Ernst

J asmine sat cross-legged at the edge of the rickety old dock, peering down into the murky, chocolate-colored water. *What if a giant jellyfish lives down there?* She frowned.

Using her hand binoculars, she laser-focused on the water below.

I don't want to get stung like my brother did last summer! she thought, shaking her head as a breeze danced with her long brown hair.

Jasmine stretched one skinny brown leg out in front of her, lowering it toward the water's surface.

Nope! I can't do it! She quickly pulled it back, causing the old dock to roll from side to side.

Jasmine's family had moved to a pole house on the river two weeks earlier. Their father was a fisherman, and they had to move closer to the ocean so he could spend more time fishing.

Jasmine cried when she said goodbye to her best friends and wondered if she would ever make new friends again.

Rowdy laughter from the pole house next door caught her attention.

Jasmine looked up just in time to see her new neighbors, Arunny and Sokha, grab each other's hand and leap off the dock into the water. They came up for air, shrieking with laughter, and scrambled up on the dock, ready to jump again.

They're not afraid of the dark water, thought Jasmine, wishing she could join in the fun.

I wouldn't be so scared if I could see what was in the water.

I wonder if Sokha and Arunny will be my new best friends, Jasmine wished.

Maybe they won't when they see what a scaredy-cat I am, she pouted.

Splash!

Jasmine jumped up.

Wiping the water from her face, she looked in both directions.

"Ha! Why don't you go make friends with Arunny and Sokha?" Chann laughed.

Jasmine stomped down the dock, her legs wide apart to keep the dock from rocking too severely.

"I can't see what's in the river!"

She shouted back at her brother, "I don't want to be stung by a jellyfish! And I'm going to tell Mom!"

"Go ahead! It was just a stupid clam shell that I threw! And you're not going to get stung by a jellyfish! Chann yelled, "They live in the ocean, not the river!" But Jasmine had already run into the house and hadn't heard him.

Jasmine sat on the floor near the table where her mom was cleaning vegetables. She could see the river below through the spaces between the worn wooden slats.

Jasmine's mom brushed her long, black hair off her face and looked down at her daughter.

"Why do you look so sad, JJ?" her mom asked tiredly.

"I miss my best friends.

Chann threw a clam shell at me.

I don't like the river!

I can't see what's in it!" Jasmine whined.

"I threw it *over* you, into the river!" Chann shouted, kicking his flip-flops off at the door.

"All right, that's enough, you two! Chann, fill the pot with water for the rice and Jasmine, go to the end of the dock and see if you can see your father's boat. He promised to save us a nice fish for dinner."

Jasmine stood up and stepped into the hot sun outside.

Shielding her eyes with her right hand, she looked down the dock, past all the pole houses, towards the ocean. There was no sign of her father's boat. With each wave that rolled in from the sea towards the pole houses, the dock rolled gently up and back down to the end, where it stopped at the lily pond.

Guessing she had time before her father got home, she walked down the dock. The lily pond was one of her favorite places. It was calm and clear at this end of the dock. You could see the fish below in the water. Warmed by the sun, the fragrance of honeysuckle filled the air. This place felt like a big hug. Jasmine remembered swimming in the pond with her brother on moving day. It was not scary because she could see what was in the water.

Suddenly, Jasmine spotted a scraggly old monkey with white whiskers leap from a low-hanging branch into the pond with a big splash! When he came up for air, a large pink lotus blossom sat perched on his head, its petals dripping with water. His smile was so ginormous that his eyes squeezed shut. Jasmine laughed with delight at the sight. And just as quickly as he appeared, he disappeared into the pond.

That monkey does not seem to be afraid of anything!

Chann said the fish fear me and will swim away when I come too close to them.

Dad said I am strong, and as long as I don't go past the last pole house, it is safe to swim in the river.

Mom said I can do anything I set my mind to.

"So why am I scared?" she yelled to the creatures of the lily pond.

Suddenly, a lily pad, with monkey arms on each side, paddled across the pond towards her!

Before she could move, the lily pad rose into the air and fell back into the water as Monkey grabbed the side of the dock and hoisted himself up, sitting beside her!

Jasmine sat, frozen, her mouth wide open.

"Hello there!' Monkey said.

"You look just like your brother, Chann!" Monkey continued, noticing her long, black hair and big brown eyes.

"Oh! You're the magical monkey my brother told me about!" Jasmine said. *I didn't believe Chann!* She thought to herself. *He's real! Monkey is right here!*

"You helped my brother be brave when he was called to the principal's office last year. It was you, wasn't it?"

"Of course, it was me! How many talking monkeys do you know?" Monkey said, waving his long, hairy arms in the air. "So, you're afraid to swim in the river, eh? I've seen you swim in the pond. You jumped in with your brother and swam across the pond on moving day. Your mom and dad were there too. Remember?" Monkey asked, scratching the top of his head.

"The river is brown now, and I can't see what's in it. A jellyfish might sting me. Or maybe a big fish will bite me!" Jasmine looked at Monkey, her eyes brimming with tears.

Monkey frowned, touching his forehead with one bony finger, and said, "Sometimes, we're afraid of things we cannot see. But with a little help, you can overcome this fear."

"What do you mean, Monkey?" Jasmine asked.

"You're forgetting to trust YOURSELF! Trust your instincts, Jasmine!"

Suddenly, Jasmine heard Chann yelling.

Being careful not to trip in the cracks in the old wood, Jasmine ran down the dock. Monkey took another route, under the dock, where the water was cool and smooth.

Chann pointed to the problem. A line from one of the fishing poles on their father's boat got tangled in an old tree branch half submerged in the middle of the river, and the tide was forcing the boat up against some big rocks.

"Chann, catch this rope!" Their father yelled over the noise of the boat bumping on the rocks. "Hold the boat so it doesn't crash into the rocks. Jasmine, I want you to wade out to the branch and pull the tangled line off."

"Jasmine, it's time to trust yourself," Monkey whispered from under the dock. "What is your gut telling you?"

"I know I am not strong enough to hold the boat," whispered Jasmine. "I need to go into the water and untangle the fishing line. I think I can do this. I just wish I could see."

"Jasmine, jump into the water like we practiced at the lily pond," Dad interrupted her. "Remember? You can do this, JJ! I believe in you!"

"You've got this!" Monkey called after her as she lowered herself into the river.

Jasmine's mom came out to see what was going on. Seeing Jasmine swim, she called out, "You can do this, Jasmine! I'm right here if you need help!"

Jasmine looked at Chann and pleaded one last time, "But. . .the jellyfish?"

"JJ, there are no jellyfish in the river! I was in the ocean when I got stung! You will be fine!" Chann yelled over his shoulder as he held on to the rope.

Jasmine looked around and, surrounded by all these words of encouragement, felt a new self-confidence push her fears away. *I will move my arms like I've seen Chann do and push the water out of my way,* Jasmine coached herself.

Moving her arms like big paddles, she pushed the water behind her. The river was not too deep, and she could stand on the soft sandy bottom. It didn't take long to reach the tangled line.

She looked back and saw that Chann was now in the water near the dock, holding onto the rope with all his might, and her father was crouching at the front of the boat, trying to keep it balanced as it rocked back and forth. He did not want to lose his catch of the day!

Jasmine pulled at the slippery mess of fishing line. After a couple of tugs, it slid off the wet branch.

"I did it!" she yelled.

At the dock, Monkey raised one skinny fist bump in the air.

"You saved the day, JJ!" her father yelled. Giving her a thumbs up, he began steering the boat across the river towards the dock.

"I'm proud of you, JJ!" called Chann as he climbed back onto the dock and joined their mom, who was clapping her hands for the job well done by all!

Jasmine turned to give Monkey a thumbs-up too, just in time to see him skipping down the dock, waving at her with one scraggly arm. His smile was so ginormous that his eyes squeezed shut!

Arunny and Sokha, who had been watching all along, clapped their hands and waved at her.

"Great job, Jasmine!" Arunny called.

 Would you like to swim to our house and play before dinner?" Sokha called.

 "Yes! Here I come!" Jasmine said, returning the wave.

Filled with a new self-confidence, Jasmine knew they would be best friends for a very long time!

Chapter 3

Sundance and Sally
The Journey to Becoming a Heart Horse
By Susan Thompson

Cock-a-doodle-do!

S argent Yawnee, the large and in charge rooster, announced at the start of the morning.

Cock-a-doodle-do!
Cock-a-doodle-do!
Cock-a-doodle-do!

What is that sound? Where is it coming from?

Sundance awoke with a start, all wonderment running through the young foal's head as he opened his eyes upon his new home.

The barnyard smelled like a combination of fresh hay and warm manure. The unique odor somehow comforted him. It was a strong smell that tickled his nostrils.

The farm sounds were new to Sundance.

He listened, and many more farm animals joined in,

oink oink,

cluck cluck,

gobble gooble,

moo moo!

The foal ran as fast as he could in circles. The mountains where he was born didn't have any of these sounds or smells

Snort!

Sundance snorted air through his nose with flared nostrils to scare away the strange noises. Standing tall with his head held high in the air, he remembered his last day with his mother and what she told him, "Be brave, my son."

Stretching his long neck out the window, Sundance could see the barnyard full of animals he had never encountered before. There was Charlotte, the muddy piglet; Sargent Yawnie, the noisy rooster and self-proclaimed leader of the farm; Tom, the fat turkey; and Della, the beautiful milk cow.

The animals gathered near the barn to get a glimpse of this new addition.

Charlotte asked the others, "What is this horse doing here?"

Tom responded, "I'm not sure, but he's very large, and his shiny coat is beautiful. He looks as though he is a young foal."

Della began to moo loudly, "Is he going to grow up to be our leader?" she wondered.

Sargent Yawnie proudly announced with fluffed feathers and the biggest, loudest frustrated crow, "That will not do because I am the leader! Everyone knows the rooster rules the roost."

All the farm animals laughed because they knew a rooster was no match for a foal, let alone a horse.

In the house, Sally throws on yesterday's clothes, thinking of her dream horse waiting for her out in the barn.

Forget the socks, she decides, as she pulls on her cowgirl boots and rushes past her mother. The back door slams. The porch steps become one big jump, and the path to the barn is a racetrack.

Dust flying in Sundance's stall made Sally concerned.

Why is he running? She thought as her steps quickened.

"Sundance!" Sally yelled, "Are you okay? You look scared!"

Just as she spoke, the resident Sargent rooster flew into the arena. Sally could see the whites of her horse's eyes as he shivered, snorted, and ran.

"I see. You are afraid of Yawnie. He is a rooster. He thinks he is the toughest, badest rooster here, but in fact, he won't hurt you."

Sally's comforting voice helped Sundance feel braver. His heart was racing, but the sound of her soft words allowed him to relax his body. Sally picked up the unhappy rooster in her arms and placed him back outside in the sunshine.

She is saving me.

Sally could see the fear going away from her mustang, Sundance's body movements which sent shivers up her spine.

Sally's mother appeared in the barn to check on her daughter. "What is going on out here, honey?"

"Mom, he was afraid of all the noises the other animals were making. When I comforted him, he changed his body language and stood there licking his lips.

"When a horse licks his lips, it means he's thinking. He trusts you and believes you will protect him. In time, he'll begin to protect you."

"When I study him, I feel what he feels, Mom." Sally smiled the biggest teeth showing smile.

The young cowgirl and her horse recognized their hearts were connecting. Sally had lost her father in a tragic accident, and Sundance's mother was captured in a wild horse round-up when he was just one hour old. The feelings of loss and loneliness were something they shared.

The rest of the farm animals were curious about the purpose of this foal. They stood and watched Sally working with Sundance.

Charlotte the piglet softly grunted instructions, "Be quiet so you don't scare the horse again."

As the animals listened, the young piglet explained, "Sundance is just a sweet baby. He was adopted by Sally because they share sad feelings about losing a parent. You must understand Sundance is a prey animal, which means predators hunt him. A horse's instinct is to be afraid, so their protection is flight."

Sally softened her movements and lowered her voice. She knew her mustang was just a baby horse with an unfortunate past. She slowly walked toward Sundance. She slumped her shoulders and slightly bent her knees so she appeared smaller.

Sundance is curious.

Why does this small human want to be so close to me? I hope it's because she wants to be friends with me.

The colors of the sky announced the evening with bright oranges and reds. Soon, it turned chilly. A warm thrill went through the cowgirl's body, feeling like a million tingling sparklers inside her heart. Time stood still while the two made memories.

Sally walked slowly around the arena. Noticing Sundance following her, she exclaimed with a piercing squeal to her mom, who was watching, "I am so excited, Mom. My mustang moves as I move."

Sally's mom responded, "This is called locking on. Your horse accepts you as someone he can trust; he believes you will protect him. This makes him want to be near you."

"Now it is time to touch Sundance and pet his soft, beautiful buckskin coat," Sally's mom continued, knowing Sundance was a young wild horse and the touch of a human was unfamiliar. She was unsure how he would react. Would Sundance jump and frighten her daughter? She instructed Sally, "If you move very slowly and be brave, the foal will be brave too. If you show fear, your horse will be nervous."

Sally bravely relaxed her body and walked slowly, step by step, closer to the foal as the two built trust. She reached her hands out and set them on the back of her horse. It was like feeling a cloud and caused excitement in her soul.

Sundance twitched his back muscles as if he were flicking off a fly.

This feels fabulous. I am not afraid. I can tell by my instincts Sally won't hurt me.

The farm animals watched as this new baby animal and Sally bonded. The more the cowgirl rubbed, the happier Sundance became.

Entering the arena with care, Sally's mom handed her a box of horse brushes. The pointed bristles felt wonderful to the foal. He began to curl his lips up and stretch out his neck in response. The cowgirl could see how his coat glistened with every stroke.

As it began to turn dark outside, Sally gathered the horse brushes. Sundance snorted and smelled the box. The curiosity of the young foal was getting the best of him.

This will be fun, he thought to himself.

He grabbed one brush in his teeth and took off running. Suddenly, the taste of fly spray on the brush made him spit it out. *Bleck, this is not a horse toy.*

Sally and her mother laughed at how silly Sundance was acting.

The foal began to buck and kick, circling Sally at a high speed.

"He is getting his yah yahs out," Sally's mother explained. "He is happy and excited and can't help himself. Horses have personality, and it looks like yours is a character."

It was time to end the lesson for the day.

Sundance needed to go to his stall, and Sally to finish her farm chores. Their brains were full of new information, and they both needed to think about things tonight.

Sally wrapped her arms around her horse's neck. She could smell the aroma of the sweat built up on Sundance's body. It smelled better than anything she had ever smelled; it was stuck in her memory forever.

"Good night, Sundance. Tomorrow is another day." She looked back at the beautiful buckskin mustang and knew how lucky she was to call him her own.

The next morning came too early for the sleepyheads. It was still dark when, right outside Sundance's stall, Sargent Yawnie loudly bellowed his cock-a-doodle-do.

Sundance, no longer afraid and completely annoyed, reached his head out the window and asked, "Why are you getting up so early? It's still very dark outside."

Sargent Yawnie ruffled his feathers and crowed again. "This is my job," he responded, "I wake up the entire farm every morning. I'm the leader, and don't' you forget it!"

A small grunting voice came from the hallway, "He always wakes us up too early," said Charlotte, the disgusted baby piglet.

Soon, the farm was buzzing with animal voices, all wishing Yawnie would stop crowing so early.

The baby chicks clucked loudly, "Will the new horse teach Sargent Yawnie what morning looks like?"

Sundance felt as if he was being accepted by the others.

Just then, another loud crow came from inside the horse's stall.

The rooster was right under Sundance's feet. Not a very safe place for him to be. The awful noise the rooster made startled the foal and made Sundance kick out in fear and begin bucking. One of his hind feet landed right square on Sargent Yawnie and sent him flying high into the arena.

The rooster shook himself off. Humiliated, he retreated to the chicken coup to regain his pride.

All the other animals cheered and laughed. They all hoped Sargent Yawnie had learned his lesson.

"I'm going to love it here," Sundance announced.

A new day rose in the barnyard as Sally came out to do her chores and pet her horse. "Everything is so peaceful out here, and it is never like that. What happened?"

All the farm animals kept quiet, especially Yawnie.

Playing with her horse more and more, Sally could understand Sundance's thinking. They communicated through feelings and body movements. As Sally made her way to her horse's side, something amazing happened. She remembered yesterday and realized there were no thoughts about the sadness from the loss of her father. This was the first day since his accident that she was happy. As Sundance snuggled his nose into her chest, it was clear he had left behind the feelings of grief from losing his mother so young.

Horse and cowgirl were joined and healed by the unity of their hearts.

Sundance has his forever home, and Sally has her Heart Horse.

Save Our Forests

Chapter 4

Amaleigha Fights for What She Believes In

Protecting the Community Forest

By Janice Pratt

Amaleigha loved to be outside. It was her happy place as long as she could remember.

Her family, too, loved nature and most years they took camping trips in the summer.

At other times, they walked on paths and trails near her house all year long.

In the spring, Amaleigha noticed many new flowers popping up and all the green leaves opening upon the trees. In the summer, she loved to stick her feet in the stream and feel the cool water tickle her toes. In the fall, the trees were bright with colored leaves. Amaleigha loved the way the colors lit up the trees with oranges and reds as if they had put on a new coat. And winter was often still and quiet. It often felt peaceful during this time.

Her favorite person to hike with was her grandma.

"Amaleigha, look over here! Do you see this spider web covered in dewdrops? It looks like diamonds!" Amaleigha's grandma called out today as they hiked.

"Amaleigha, listen to the bluebirds singing this morning. Let's make our morning song!" And off she would dance, and singing at the top of her lungs,

> *"Morning is here,*
> *The sun is shining,*
> *And the breeze is blowing,*
> *life is sweet!"*

Today, on her walk with her grandma, their favorite trail had an orange tape across the path and a big sign planted in the middle of the trail.

COMMUNITY MEETING TONIGHT!

Location: Town Hall

Time: 7 p.m.

Topic: Building project for a new parking lot.

Come and join the planning session!

"Grandma, how can they build a parking lot in this beautiful forest?" Amaleigha asked. "All the animals will lose their homes! All the trees will be gone. This makes me so mad!" Amaleigha said as she clenched her fists tight.

"Well, Amaleigha, I guess we have to go to that meeting tonight! They need to know what our community will lose if the forest is replaced with a concrete parking lot! Let's go get our facts together!"

With a purposeful stride, hand in hand, Amaleigha and her grandma walked toward the library.

Side by side, they burst through the library doors, both doors slamming on the wall behind them. The loud bang brought Miss Mabel out of the room behind the desk, and with raised eyebrows, she surveyed Amaleigha and Grandma, striding toward the desk.

"Miss Mabel, we need to find out some facts! Did you know our town wants to build a new parking lot in the forest? And there is a meeting tonight. I need to know ways that nature helps people and the animals, too!" Amaleigha spewed the words out in a rush of air.

For the next two hours, they read and made notes and talked to others at the library about their project.

It seemed that the more people they talked to, the more they realized that not many knew about this new parking lot plan. When they heard about it, they became just as upset as Amaliegha and her grandma.

Everyone they talked to promised to spread the word.

"Nature lovers are uniting, Grandma," said Amaleigha when they finally headed home with tons of notes. Now, they just needed to organize all they'd learned.

Amaleigha and her grandma busted through Amaleigha's front door with a bang that got everyone in the house's attention. Soon, Amaleigha's mom and dad were helping out, and even Amaleigha's big brother threw out some great ideas.

Amaleigha grabbed their final notes, cleared her throat with a little cough, and began to read a speech she had prepared:

"Forests are important places for the life of our planet but also for the health of our community. They give us fresh air to breathe. They are homes to deer, mice, insects, bees, and birds. They help keep people healthy by giving us places to exercise. Walking is good for your heart and lungs and makes you happy. More concrete and cars in our town will make it hotter and will pollute the air. We need to protect our nature.

Let's vote for a happy, healthy life—for the trees, for the animals, and for us!"

Grandma, Mom, Dad, and even Al clapped and cheered.

"Amaleigha, you have to say all of that tonight at the meeting!" Grandma said as she gave Amaleigha a big hug.

When Amaleigha, Grandma, and her family walked into the community meeting, Grandma and Amaliegha noticed many of the people they had talked to today were also seated in the town hall auditorium. Her whole family took seats and waited for the city council to start the meeting.

The city planner, Mr. Benson, started the meeting, "Our town is growing, and we need to bring in more business to accommodate this growth. I propose that we take this unused piece of woods and provide a place for people to park near shopping."

Mr. Benson continued for the next 20 minutes talking about new businesses, growth, and buildings until Amaleigha was completely lost in his words. Her mind created images of concrete buildings lining the forest path and cars parked where the tall oak trees used to be. She imagined the animal homes covered with concrete. A tear slipped silently down her cheek as the images swirled in her mind.

"Thank you, Mr. Bension, for this plan," said a council member. "We would now like to open the floor for suggestions."

Many people Amaleigha knew asked questions like:

"How much will the project cost?"

"What new businesses will be added to the community?"

"How will this help our community?"

Finally, Mr. Benson started to wrap up the meeting by asking, "Alright, are there any more comments from the community?"

Grandma gently nudged Amaleigha. Slowly, she raised her hand.

"Yes, young lady?" called Mr. Benson. "What would you like to say?" His voice had a bit of a smirk to it as if he couldn't believe that someone Amaleigha's age could have anything important to say at all!

Amaleigha stood up with her notes in her hand. "My name is Amaleigha Johansen, and I live here with my family. My grandma and I walk on the trail to town almost every day."

Amaleigh then launched into the speech she had prepared and practiced in front of her family.

When she finished, she looked directly at Mr. Benson and added, "Let's vote for a happy, healthy life for the trees, for the animals, and for us!"

The community audience burst out in applause that lasted so long that the mayor finally called for everyone to be seated.

"Order! Order! Ladies and gentlemen, thank you for your questions and comments. I can see how important our natural resources are to many of you. Hopefully, we can continue to improve our community while also protecting the outdoor spaces. I think before we make any big decisions, we need to look at some options for our growth plan and figure out how to make our natural resources an important part of our community." And with that, the meeting was adjourned.

Many neighbors came up and hugged Amaleigha, along with her grandma, who was right beside her.

As Amaleigha's grandma twirled her around, she gushed out, "It wouldn't have happened if you hadn't spoken up, Amaleigha! I don't know anyone as gutsy as you! I can't wait to see what you tackle next," she laughed as she gave her another big hug.

Amaleigha, her grandma, and her family all took the forest path home, splashing in rain puddles along the way, running and laughing as the birds joined in with their songs.

For now, they knew their animal friends were safe.

Chapter 5

Building Your Life T.E.A.M.
By Samara Ena Minichiello

The man with the big blue square glasses did it again!

He taught me a new way to apply my power to make my days even happier!

He taught me T.E.A.M., which stands for *Trust Each other And Myself.*

And I get to decide who I want on the most important team of all, **my life team.**

When I have problems or things that are difficult for me to understand, I like to talk to this man with the big blue glasses. He previously taught me my power to *catch my negative thoughts before they ruin my day.* I learned I have the power to choose which of my thoughts are welcome to stay. Today, I'm having problems trusting kids in school who aren't contributing to projects as much as I do.

This was how he taught me a new way to apply my power.

"Is this how it's always going to be?" I asked the man in the big blue square glasses.

"How is what going to be, Daniel?" He asked me to clarify.

"I don't know, like whenever I work in a team, I have to do everything?" I said, concerned.

"What else do you believe is true of your team members?" he asked.

"I believe they don't try as hard as me and don't care. I can't trust they will do their part," I told the man.

He leaned closer and said, "Oh, you mentioned **trust.** Tell me more about what you mean."

"I can't depend on them to get their work done correctly or on time, so I can't trust them. I can only trust myself," I shared.

"Yes," I responded.

"Then is it possible to trust the team members you get assigned to on school projects?" he asked.

"Maybe," I hesitated, then continued, "Well, because I have proof it could work. It took me and my soccer team time to trust each other, but we do now."

"It does take time to trust. Do you give your assigned project team members a chance to be trusted?" he asked.

"We have only a couple of hours to accomplish a task, so I don't have enough time to trust them. I can only trust myself to do good work," I answered.

He was not satisfied with my answer, so he pressed more, "But do they trust *you*?"

"Do they trust *me*?" I questioned back.

He wiggled in his chair and replied, "Yes, they are assigned to you. What if they are still deciding if they can trust you and won't have to carry the load themselves because you won't do your part?"

"They *have to* give me a chance to show I will do my part," I felt entitled to say.

In a calm voice, the man said, "Yes, Daniel. So how do you think they trust you?"

Sitting more upright in his chair, he replied, "Interes
We can use your power to change your thoughts in this insta
Want to try it?"

"Of course! I LOVE using the previous power you taught m
I responded enthusiastically.

He made one of his side smirk smiles, then returned to a serio
face, saying, "Okay, let's slightly switch gears here. How's socc
been for you?"

"Uh, soccer? It's been amazing! My team is undefeated!
I confidently replied.

"Wow!" he responded. "How does that make you feel? Where
do you feel it in your body?"

"It makes me feel unstoppable and strong. I feel it in my chest,
back, shoulders, arms, and hands. I feel uplifted and taller, like
after I just scored a goal!" I told him.

He nodded and replied, "Yes, the feelings and sensations your
body are giving you are a sign of strength. You even sat up taller
more expanded as you were speaking. Did you notice that?"

"I do now that you mentioned it to me," I said with a crooke
smile.

"As part of your soccer team, you feel unstoppable and stror
right? So, you have experience being on a team and trusting yc
team members and yourself simultaneously?" he question
further.

This calmed my response, and I answered, "They may have seen my work and know I'm a good team member."

"But what if they have no experience teaming up with you or know nothing about you and your work?" he asked.

"They have to give me a chance to show them!" I demanded. *Ugh*. "If they don't know how I work but allow me to give them a chance to see what I can offer the team, they can build trust in my abilities."

"What if you gave your new team members the same chance and safe space to show you?" He asked.

"Safe space?" I responded with confusion.

I hope he explains this one, I thought.

And he did, "Yes, like we have here. A space where we can be open, judgment-free, kind, and understanding. Do you think you could offer this to your team members?"

"Yes, I guess I could," I replied.

He continued to share his thoughts, saying, "It *could* take pressure off you believing you must do everything and give each one of you a chance to become a real team. Let me teach you an acronym for T.E.A.M., which may help.

The T stands for Trust.
E stands for Each other.
A stands for And,
and M stands for Myself."

I liked this. *Trust Each other And Myself.* "I do feel less pressure knowing this is an option," I said.

"Good, because it's a belief you have the power to choose whenever you're on a team. As you get older, you'll find the ability to trust others is essential. But unfortunately, you'll experience people who come into your life who you cannot trust, and *you* decide if they will be part of **your Life T.E.A.M.**" he explained.

"My Life T.E.A.M.?" I slowly questioned.

"Yes, these people in your life have your back, and you have theirs." He continued, "A Life T.E.A.M. is a collection of family members, friends, pets, neighbors, coworkers, therapists, doctors, coaches, mentors, teachers, and anyone else who adds happiness and value to your life. Their character and actions demonstrate they can be trusted. Sometimes, we believe and trust people at their word and find out later they haven't been telling the truth. We get to decide if we want them on our Life T.E.A.M. If you stay honest, many people will like you on their Life T.E.A.M."

"Can you start to see how this works and why learning how to trust people and giving them a chance to be good team members is essential?" he asked me.

"Yes, I never thought of that," I admitted. "So, my classmates assigned to projects with me, my soccer teammates, and my life teammates should all get the same courtesy they give me to show them I'm trustworthy, and we can be a good team together?" I confirmed.

"You got it!" he declared with a huge smile.

"And if you experience a situation where people aren't holding their weight or aren't being honest, you can know it's that specific situation or individual. It doesn't mean everyone will be like them in the future. You can allow people a safe space to show their intentions through actions, not just words. You'll also see some of the team members you get assigned to on school projects or on your soccer team turn into friends you may one day invite to join your Life T.E.A.M. The point is, some people will be in your life for only a **season**, like a school project, a **reason,** like to teach you an important lesson, **or for your whole life.**"

"Wow, the people I'm assigned to on teams could be there for a short season, for a specific reason, or to be part of my Life T.E.A.M.? So cool!" I shouted.

"Yes, it *is* cool," he agreed. "And you may get to be a part of their Life T.E.A.M., too! We all need a Life T.E.A.M. to become our best selves."

"Look, Daniel, some people won't make it to your Life T.E.A.M., which is perfectly fine. Only the people you choose can be on it. It's the special few who will be on your Life T.E.A.M. because there's a mutual safe space of trust, and you will trust yourself to know these are the right people." He went on to ask, "Has this new insight been helpful?"

"Yes, extremely," I happily confirmed. "I understand now I may not have allowed team members a chance for me to trust them and their abilities. Instead, I judged them based on others I had worked with in the past, which was unfair. I believed everyone was the same and it would never change. I see now how that puts a lot of pressure on me. Working as a team requires trust in my team members and myself. I'll remember the acronym T.E.A.M.—Trust Each other And Myself. I need to work on giving people a safe space without judgment. I'll pay attention to people's actions, not just their words. And if I stay trustworthy, people will want me on their Life T.E.A.M."

"Umm, does this mean you're on my Life T.E.A.M.?" I asked shyly.

He looked directly into my sinking brown eyes and asked, "Do I provide a safe space for you? Do you trust me? Do you feel happier after we interact?"

"Yes, to all!" I perked up with confidence.

He then softened his message to say, "If you want me to be a part of your Life T.E.A.M., I would be honored to accept your invitation," he then paused to watch my reaction. I was happy.

"Next time we talk, let's discuss who else is on your Life T.E.A.M. What do you think about that?" he asked.

"Wow, that would be so much fun!" I said excitedly.

"Then consider it done! Until next time, remember to use your power and apply it to T.E.A.M.

He then tested me, "What does T stand for?"

"TRUST."

He continued, "What does E stands for?"

"EACH OTHER."

In a louder tone, he asked, "A stands for?"

"AND."

Determined, the man asked, "M stands for?"

"MYSELF!" I joyfully ended.

I've SO got this building your Life T.E.A.M. thing!

*

I feel grateful for the man in the big blue square glasses and all the wisdom he has shared with me. I think everyone needs someone to look up to for help navigating through life's challenges. I don't think we can do it alone.

Chapter 6

Caroline, the Queen of Recess, Finds Her Voice

By Meredith Speir

"What I REALLY want to do is NOT have recess!" said Caroline to her best friend Olivia when she asked what she wanted to do out on the playground.

"I think I'd rather work on math than go outside today!" Caroline continued as she looked for her math book, which was stuffed deep inside her backpack.

"I wish I were the queen of the school then I could decide what should happen to those mean girls who bully us at recess. I could proclaim that Rachel and Amanda be moved to another school, far, far away! They are so mean—the meanest!"

"I'm going to play four square," Olivia said calmly.

"Well, I'm not!" Caroline exclaimed.

Caroline is in her last year of elementary school—fourth grade, which can be extremely tough, accompanied by some VERY BIG FEELINGS.

School has been difficult this year. There are so many tests, and the mean girls, Rachel and Amanda, have recently decided to pick on and poke fun at Caroline and Olivia.

It's a few weeks before Thanksgiving, and recess is getting colder by the day. On this cold and wintry November morning, Caroline walked to school with her white beanie hat, warm gloves, and a puffy purple coat, which she adored.

At 10 a.m., Mr. Kilby, their homeroom teacher, announces, "It's time to go out for our first recess of the day! Bundle up! It's cold."

Caroline looks anxiously around the classroom.

She grabs her coat, gloves, and beanie out of her cubby.

The thoughts in her head begin to swirl around and around. There was a sick feeling in the pit of her stomach where this feeling had been happening before recess more and more often.

Oh no. It's already time for recess?

Yesterday, Rachel and Amanda were so mean to me. When I got out in four square, they called me dumb and told me I was a 'waste of space.'

Four square used to be Caroline's favorite activity to do at recess. It was a game where four boxes for four players were drawn on the blacktop with chalk. When playing, you had to hit a ball into another player's square after it had bounced only once in their own square. This game that was once fun really seemed to have gotten out of hand with Rachel and Amanda leading it and calling people names, poking fun at anyone who got out, and using hurtful and unkind words.

What do I want to do at recess? Caroline asked herself. *Because I'm forced to go to recess, I will not play four square.*

Mr. Kilby's fourth-grade students all made a line at the door of her classroom. The mean girls, Rachel and Amanda, were staring at all the girls in the class, whispering and smirking.

*I hate recess this year. Those girls are mean. I am **not** going to talk to them. I'll play on the swings today. I'll do anything to stay away from them.* Caroline thought as they walked through the hallways of the school.

The doors leading out to the playground flung open, and the mean girls were the first ones out the door, headed straight for four square.

The air was cold, and the sun hid behind the clouds.

Caroline walked nervously towards the swings. None of her friends wanted to swing today. Most of the kids were playing four square. She got on the swing and began to pump her legs to go as high as she could.

She noticed that her stomach still felt uneasy. No one from her class was on the swings, just the first graders.

Oh no, here they come.

The mean girls had left the four square game and were headed straight to the swings. They were walking fast, pointing, and laughing. All of the swings were taken by a few first graders and Caroline. Caroline tried to pretend that she did not see the girls, but they stood in front of her and stared her down until she looked at them.

"Hey, do you know you're swinging with all the little first graders? How embarrassing!" Rachel yelled.

"No one wants to play with you. You're such a loser and were the very first one out yesterday in four square. I guess that is why you're over here swinging by yourself at recess," Amanda said.

Caroline's eyes began to fill up with tears. The tears ran down her cheeks as she dragged her feet on the ground in an effort to stop swinging and get away from the girls. The swing came to a complete stop, but the thoughts in her head did not stop. She got off the swing, and as she walked toward the bench, Rachel ran behind her and snatched her white beanie off her head. Rachel and Amanda skipped away, laughing and throwing her beanie back and forth.

Mr. Kilby, who hadn't seen this bullying, blew the whistle and raised his hand, which signaled that recess was over.

Thank goodness that is over!

What do I say to Rachel and Amanda? I have no clue.

How am I going to get my beanie back?

Mommy tells me to use my voice, but I don't know what to say to stand up for myself.

Olivia spent the rest of the school day trying to convince Caroline to play four square. Her efforts were unsuccessful. Caroline was quiet and reserved for the remainder of the school day. At one point, Mr. Kilby asked her, "What's wrong? Are you okay?" She didn't want to talk and avoided conversations with almost everyone for the rest of the day. The bus ride home from school was quiet and lonely.

Caroline's mommy met her at the front door of their house. She knew something was very wrong from the look on Caroline's face. There were tears in Caroline's eyes, her brow was furrowed, and her lip corners were pulled down.

"How was your day?" she asked.

"It was terrible!" Caroline shouted. "I do not want to go back tomorrow!"

"What happened, honey?"

"What didn't happen? I can't even play four square anymore because Rachel and Amanda make fun of me. When I decided to swing by myself, they followed me, made fun of me, and called me a loser. I am a loser, and they stole my beanie!"

"It's hard to find the words to say when someone bullies us or hurts our feelings. How does it make you feel when the girls talk to you like they do?"

"I feel angry and left out. I wish I were the queen of the school who could make those girls disappear."

"Hmm, what if *you* could be *The Queen of Recess* and find your voice on the playground? How would it feel to stand up for yourself and tell people how you feel?"

"I don't know if I can do that."

"Well, I *know* that you *can* do that! A queen manages her energy wisely and picks her battles. If a queen is getting bullied, she relies on her confidence to stand up for herself and her friends. Did you know that in the game of chess, the queen is the only piece in the game that can move any number of squares in any direction?"

"Come on, Mom. I don't know how to play chess!"

"You don't have to know how to play chess. You *do* have the opportunity to find your voice and stand up for what is right."

"I will try tomorrow, Mommy."

"I know that you can do it."

Caroline was able to get a good night's sleep that night. She woke up the next morning and was determined to speak up and face the mean girls. When she arrived at school, she smiled and said hello to her teacher and friends. After a quick math lesson, it was time for recess.

"What do you want to do today?" Olivia asked.

"I'm playing four square with you. I'm not going to let those mean girls tell me what to do at recess anymore," Caroline announced.

"Awesome! Let's go," Olivia shouted.

By the time Caroline and Olivia arrived at the four square game, Rachel and Amanda were already on the blacktop heckling the girls that got out of the game.

Caroline and Olivia got into the game rather quickly. The ball was coming hard and fast towards Olivia. She tried to hit the ball, but it went out of bounds.

"Out of bounds!" Amanda shouted.

"Olivia, you are fat and ugly, and you stink at this game," Rachel snickered.

Olivia walked off the blacktop crying. Caroline was still in the game and remembered the conversation she and her mommy had last night. She took a deep breath and reminded herself that queens are confident and wise.

"Stop it, Rachel and Amanda," Caroline exclaimed. "No one deserves to be treated the way you two treat the girls in our class! It's not okay to call us names and be unkind. That's not how to treat people on the playground."

Rachel and Amanda looked at each other and genuinely seemed shocked by what they heard. No one had ever stood up to the two of them.

"Also, whoever has my beanie needs to give it back to me, or I will talk to Mr. Kilby," Caroline announced.

TWEEEET. The whistle sounded. Caroline walked back inside with Olivia.

"Don't pay any attention to those two," Caroline said to Olivia.

"Thanks for sticking up for me," Oliva remarked.

"That is what friends are for," Caroline shared.

As Caroline approached her desk, she noticed that her white beanie was on her chair. She smiled and was proud of what she did at recess, and from that day on, Caroline became The Queen of Recess. She found her voice on the playground and stood up for herself and her friend. Somedays, her voice was louder than others, but she really liked the sound of it.

Chapter 7

Knocking It Out of the Park
Three T's for a Smoother Transition
By Dr. Heidi MacAlpine

Shvoooooooooooooooooooo!

Like a vacuum sucking the chaos out of my brain, I hear my mom's caring but firm voice echoing in the background, guiding me to a safe and calm space. Her familiar words fill my head, distracting me from the chaos bouncing inside of it, lighting up neurons at the speed of light—like fireworks going off on the Fourth of July.

"Shepppppppppppppppppp.

"The *three T's*sssssssssssssssss.

"Shep!"

The three Ts have helped me survive and thrive in more ways than I can count on my chubby and strong hands. My team, with my mom in the lead, and my backpack with its survival sensory tools by my side (and on my back!), keeps me feeling where my feet are so I am grounded, committed, and focused to accomplishing anything!

Sometimes, all it takes is one person to help make sense of difficult situations during the unexpected and overwhelming times that pull me into a tailspin. The unexpected can shake my thinking up, confuse me, and my thoughts shift to the image of a kite flying high in the sky, flapping its tail with uncontrollable spins and swirls.

I find myself reacting the same way as the kite when I do not use my survival tools, and as a consequence of flying too high, apologize for doing things that create havoc in the lives of my friends, family, and classmates.

In case you didn't know, the three T's stand for:

TAKE the time,
TRACK the threat, and
TAKE note or TALK it out.

You just never know when you will need these survival tools and who will be on your team to cheer you on and encourage you to make it to each base on and off the field.

Now that I've turned ten, so much more is expected of me, and I am supposed to know how to handle challenging situations on my own. Not everyone understands how my brain and body work, but my mom, family, and occupational therapist all do. My mom and occupational therapist have a way of putting a positive spin on a tailspin. It isn't always easy, especially when I get nervous and excited, or things don't go as originally planned. But the three Ts help to prevent or pull me out of a tailspin and help me realize that most things are not a big threat. No tigers are chasing me! Ha ha!

Boom, boom! Snap, crackle, sizzle, pop, boom, boom!

Here I go again!

It isn't easy to slow my mind and body down.

The neurons in my brain fire at the speed of light, and my body gets jittery just thinking about what is expected of me at the baseball championship game tonight. Sometimes it happens so quickly.

The three 'Ts! I remember. I remember.

The first step is taking a breath. The Lazy Eight breathing technique is my favorite. It slows the flying images in my head down and the thumping and pumping of my heart.

Breathe and squeeze! Breathe and squeeze!

It doesn't take long this time before I am able to control my emotions, thoughts, and actions, and it feels great!

 Hummmmmmmmmmmmmmmmm.

I feel my Ferrari engine slowing down to a deep purr, and I am less jittery. Sometimes, all it takes is one person to help make sense of difficult situations during unexpected and overwhelming times. I feel myself smile. This time it was me. I've been practicing keeping my body and mind fine-tuned for the championship game tonight—no tail spinning nor firecrackers going off in my head.

Snap, crackle, sizzle, pop!

I run around in my room with my legs and arms in constant motion like a tail-spinning kite in heavy wind. I thought I had this under control. Something pauses me long enough to stop my thoughts from whipping around and register three familiar words: "Three Ts, Shep!"

I can see my mom's worried, blurred face at my bedroom door and hear her concerned voice loud and clear, "You've got this; choose your tools," my mom says before leaving the doorway.

TRACK the threat, TRACK the threat.

No, this isn't an emergency. I've got this! My mind is playing tricks on me. I practice my calming techniques with another tool to get me in the zone. I feel for a familiar rubber but squishy toy in my backpack, Mr. Green-eyed Frogman, one of my favorite calming toys. It's a toy that provides pressure to my hands and relaxes me the more I squeeze it. It focuses my attention on my hand and the toy, and for some reason, I feel calmer. Hummmmmmmmmmmmmmmm.

Snap, crackle, pop, boom, boom!

I work hard to stay focused and relaxed for tonight. I am seriously fighting to stay calm and in control. I desperately need deflating before fireworks set off in my head again. I feel better when my brain and body are humming and purring.

CLUNK!

OUCH!

My head took a big hit on the bedpost because of the chaos and excitement flying around in my head and body.

The three 'Ts'! I hear myself saying in my head. *You've got this!*

I need to prepare for the big game, be in the right mindset, and practice being on the field! The Tigers are in the playoffs, and I am the first baseman. I need to stay focused and on my 'A' game. The excitement is overwhelming me! The Ferrari motor is revving up! I need to remember my three T's. I can do this! I'm worth it! My mind envisions my colorful and organized chart on the wall next to my bed. *I need to be in control for the big game. The Tigers can win the baseball championship with this right mindset.*

SLAM! BANG!

Before I know it, I'm slamming my bedroom door and my eyes are darting left and right and up and down in search of my sensory chart. The colorful and organized chart is on the left side of my bed. I need a moment to reorganize my thoughts! My eyes fix on the colorful picture of a Mr. Green-eyed Frogman on the chart. Yes! I grab the familiar shape from my backpack. Squeezing it with all my strength, I laugh out loud. I'm hoping by squeezing the energy right out of Frogman that I squeeze the energy right out of my body.

Closing my eyes, I imagine the symbol of a lazy eight as I breathe in and out three times.

I imagine Frogman's bright green eyes bulging out of his head.

I open my eyes; it's exactly how I pictured it would look.

You may not understand this, but the deep pressure from squeezing Frogman somehow relaxes me and puts me at ease.

TAKE time to breathe,
TRACK how big a threat this is,
and TAKE note of what works.
This works!

I won't be able to bring Frogman to the game, but I will be able to squeeze my hand during the game as if I was squeezing it.

Survival-game backpack checked!

Out the door in the car!

Finally here!

I patiently wait, focused and alert in my ready position, for the last play of the night. The bases are loaded, and I breathe slowly and deeply while pushing my cleats into the dirt as I exhale to stay in the moment on my 'A' game. I still feel some fireworks going off in my brain and the THUMP, THUMPING in my chest. My motor and thoughts begin to feel like a ninety-mile-an-hour baseball making contact with a bat.

Take the time, track the threat, and take note or talk it out, Shep. My mind hears my mom's soft and supporting words.

I squeeze my left hand into the tightest fist with a lazy eight breath. I ground myself with the pressure of the cleats into the soles of my feet and feel the pressure of the fingernails indenting my left palm. I smell the dirt and then the fresh grass. This keeps me in the moment.

CRACK!

The batter hit a ground ball moving at ninety miles an hour to first base. I inhale for a count of four, push my cleats deeper into the dirt, and squeeze my free hand as I crotch down to catch the ball.

SMACK!

The sting of the first ball numbs my hand. I give the glove one quick squeeze to prevent the ball from escaping my grasp. I hear the cheers from the bleachers and feel the hugs and pats on my back from my teammates. We won! I will remember this moment forever.

After the game, I fly up the stairs and into my room. SLAM! I hear the door close as I dive into my soft, comfortable, Yankee-striped chair in the corner of my bedroom to write about my day, my tools, and how I helped myself knock it out of the park with my survival tools. I feel myself sinking into the softness of the chair even further as I sense something I haven't felt in a long time. There is a warmth in the center of my chest, and it feels good.

I was able to take control of my emotions and actions to make a difference in my life and my teams. My team of people know me and supports me to think and use my tools to be more organized and less chaotic, and you know what? It feels better than having to apologize for doing or saying the wrong thing. It just makes my life easier.

I realized that anything can be overcome! There is a solution when we stop to listen and use our three T's for a smoother transition to stay on your A game.

Imagine what's possible with the right tools, focus, and commitment to be a team player. You and I can knock it out of the park, whether that's in sports or the game of life. I can do it! I am braver than I think. "You can do it, too! We can be the champion in our own game."

NEW ADVENTURES

Dear passengers,

We are now 'bout to enter uncharted waters.

Hold tight, 'cause it may be an extremely wonderfully bumpy yet thrilling adventurous ride as we turn the pages into our new *Brave Kids* adventures!

Each story which is 'bout to unfold is yet to be told. So, as we journey ahead, be bold and behold as we cross the marvelous threshold!

Chapter 8

Bunder and Muggermuch
A Unique Friendship
Between a Monkey and a Crocodile
By Dr. Shelley Astrof

At the heart of this tale are gems to uncover,
What's unseen but felt is what you'll discover.
Your heart's delight is a gift to behold,
Now, let's read the story, and all will be told.

n a lush jungle beside a glistening river, a clutch of cream-colored eggs was hatching. Amidst the squeaking and grunting, baby crocodiles cracked open their shells.

Max, the boss, popped out first. Next came Matt, the brazen, Millie, the bumptious, followed by Mark, the bully. Last to hatch was the mild-mannered Muggermuch.

Muggermuch looked like his siblings, with his grey-green scaly body and toothy grin, yet an uneasiness stirred within him. Unlike his fellow hatchlings, who reveled in rowdy, ruthless behavior, which scared him, Muggermuch concealed a gentleness that clashed with the expected crocodile conduct.

Despite loving his siblings, the idea of being different was unbearable.

I'll have to run away from these problems to find peace, he thought.

Maneuvering through the jungle waters, Muggermuch felt the uneasiness weighing heavily on his beating crocodile heart. Exhausted and hungry, he rested under the shade of a tree. Muggermuch was about to doze off when he heard a voice.

"Hi there!"

Looking around, Muggermuch wondered, *where's that sprightly voice coming from?*

"Look up. It's me, Bunder, your friendliest monkey in the jungle. Who are you?"

"I'm Muggermuch, a crocodile. I'm tired and hungry from all my traveling."

"I've got mangos here in this tree. Would you like some?"

"What are Mangos?" Muggermuch asked.

"Mangos are slices of sunshine, bursting with juicy-sweetness and painted in bright colors of joy!" Bunder explained. "Open your mouth, and I'll toss you some. I'm a pretty good shot."

Muggermuch's eyes widened with delight. Seeing the brightly-colored mangos, his mouth opened even wider.

"You've got quite the toothy grin there," Bunder chuckled as he tossed mango after mango with incredible precision. Muggermuch caught every mango that was pitched.

"YUMMY! These mangos are delicious! I've never tasted anything like this," he remarked.

"What brought you to this part of the jungle?" asked Bunder.

"I was swimming away from my problems. I couldn't fit in with my rowdy, ruthless siblings, who I'm still afraid of. I'm kind and gentle, so un-crocodile-like. They always made me feel like something was wrong with me," confided Muggermuch, "But my problems came with me."

"Can you show me your problems?" Bunder asked with interest, "I can't see them."

Muggermuch thought before answering. "I carry my problems in my heart; they're very heavy. You can't see them with your eyes or weigh them with a scale."

"Problems are carried in one's heart?" Bunder reflected. "They're not seen with eyes or weighed with a scale? How curious."

As days drifted by, their friendship flourished, brimming with joy, mangos, and endless talks.

"What does the jungle look like from the water?" inquired the ever-curious Bunder.

"If you hop on my back, I'll show you," Muggermuch offered.

A monkey on a crocodile's back. Can I trust him? Bunder wondered.

Sensing his unease, Muggermuch asked, "What's going on?"

"Can I trust you?" Bunder blurted.

Muggermuch smiled his toothy smile, "We're best friends. Of course, you can trust me. I'll stay close to the shore so you can jump off my back if you feel uneasy."

Bunder took a leap of faith and jumped on Muggermuch's back.

As they sailed the jungle waters, the duo sang at the top of their voices,

"B.F.F. Best-Friends-Forever! B.F.F. Best-Friends-Forever!"

All the jungle creatures rushed to the shore to see what the commotion was about. They couldn't believe their eyes. Word of this extraordinary friendship between a monkey and a crocodile spread like wildfire. When the news reached the ears of Muggermuch's crocodile family, they were flabbergasted. They summoned Muggermuch to come and tell them all about it, and Muggermuch accepted their invitation.

Eager to support his friend, Bunder prepared a basket of delicious mangos as a gift for Muggermuch's family.

"What's in the basket?" asked Millie when Muggermuch arrived.

Not even a 'hello,' how rude. They're only interested in what's in the basket.

"This is a gift for you from my friend, the monkey." Muggermuch opened the basket and watched as their crocodile eyes feasted on the brightly-colored mangos. They had never seen mangos before.

"Hey, Muggermuch, how'd you get these treats?" Mark asked.

"Where do mangos come from?" Matt chimed in.

They all spoke at once, making quite the kafuffle. They had so many questions.

"Is the rumor true? Are you friends with a monkey?" Max asked.

Muggermuch nodded in agreement.

While feasting on the delicious mangos, his siblings jumped to a typical crocodile-like conclusion. "If his monkey friend eats these delicious mangos, then the heart of this monkey must be delectable." They all nodded hungrily in agreement.

"Muggermuch, you must bring your monkey friend to us so we can taste his delicious heart," demanded Max.

Muggermuch was horrified at this suggestion—bringing his dear friend to be a snack for his family. Influenced by his crocodile company and fearful of his siblings, he agreed to bring Bunder to them.

Swimming the jungle waters after his visit, Muggermuch reflected. *When I carried the heavy mangos, my heart was so light, I paddled so fast. But now, I have no mangos to carry, yet my heart is so heavy I can hardly keep afloat. My problems follow me wherever I go.*

When Muggermuch saw Bunder again, he was overwhelmed by the joy and playfulness his friend radiated.

"Were they happy to see you? Did they like the mangos?" Bunder was eager to hear about Muggermuch's family visit.

With a heavy heart, Muggermuch spoke about his visit and reluctantly mentioned, "My family would like to meet you."

Muggermuch's heart was torn in two.

How can I do what the crocodiles ask?

How can I NOT do what the crocodiles ask?

Bunder sensed something was amiss but couldn't put his finger on it, yet he decided to support his friend. "I'd be delighted to meet them."

With a big basket of mangos, Bunder and Muggermuch set off for crocodile country; still, Bunder couldn't shake his feelings of misgiving. "Muggermuch, what are you uneasy about?"

Far from the safety of the shore, Muggermuch, filled with guilt, sheepishly revealed, "My family wants to taste your heart."

Quick-witted Bunder quipped, "Why didn't you tell me this earlier? Monkeys don't carry their hearts with them. I left mine at home. Let's go get it!"

Back to the shore they went to pick up Bunder's heart. When they reached his home, Bunder leaped to the highest branch.

"Give me a moment, Muggermuch," he called down.

Knowing his friend's heart was influenced by the crocodiles, Bunder paused, closed his eyes, and took a deep breath.

In a flash, he knew exactly what to do.

With this outrageous ingenuity, Bunder tossed a wooden box to his friend. "Here's where I keep my heart. Open it."

Muggermuch opened the lid and looked inside. "I'm looking at me in a mirror. What does this mean, Bunder?"

"It means *you* are in my heart," replied Bunder, his eyes twinkling with affection.

Muggermuch was stunned. Tears welled up in his eyes, and his massive throat choked up. He felt so many things at once. Bunder showed him the difference between his own pure heart and a heart influenced by crocodiles. Muggermuch understood that problems will come and go; the strength to face them lies in embracing his own uniqueness.

Bunder and Muggermuch's friendship became legendary. They were quite the spectacle—a monkey on the back of a crocodile spreading good cheer to all. They were the talk of the jungle.

When Muggermuch didn't return, Max, Matt, Millie, and Mark decided to pay him a visit. They were bamboozled at the sight of a crocodile laughing and sharing mangos with a monkey.

"Muggermuch, why didn't you bring the monkey's heart to us?" Max asked.

"Where is it?" Mark demanded.

"We were expecting to taste the monkey's heart," Matt blurted.

Muggermuch grinned, "Hearts are meant to be kept safe—inside."

They were puzzled.

Muggermuch remembered Bunder's heart-box. "My monkey friend keeps both our hearts in this special box."

Millie was confused, "Hearts in boxes? That's strange."

Mark hungrily said, "Can we taste both hearts?"

With patience and gentleness, Muggermuch said, "Here they are, but these hearts aren't for tasting; they're for sharing. They grow bigger and bigger the more they are shared."

Placing the box in front of them, Muggermuch said, "Stand close together as you open it."

The crocodiles opened the box and gazed at their reflections in the mirror.

"We're looking at ourselves. What does this mean? We were expecting a tasty snack inside."

Muggermuch said with genuine kindness and affection, "*You* are all in our hearts."

The crocodiles were caught off guard. They thought long and hard about the idea of keeping hearts safe—inside, a kind of heart that grows bigger the more it's shared.

That evening, as the stars twinkled above the glistening river, the crocodiles gathered by the water's edge. They couldn't shake the feeling they were missing something crucial about hearts and friendship, and they were keen to learn.

Their crocodile hearts started tingling with warmth and sweetness—inside.

Matt spoke up, "What if it's not about tasting hearts but about the sweetness they hold?"

Millie nodded, "Remember the mangos Muggermuch brought us? They were sweeter than anything we'd ever tasted."

Mark added, "Maybe the sweetness isn't the heart itself but the kindness it holds."

"If sweetness was in the kindness found in the heart, then maybe we can find it too!" Max said.

A warm gust of friendship and kindness flooded their crocodile hearts, which opened them to new friendships—not only with other crocodiles but with animals of all species. They no longer measured the strength of a crocodile by how many hearts were eaten; they measured their strength by how many hearts were touched by the sweetness of kindness and friendship.

Kindness and friendship made their hearts grow bigger and bigger, so much bigger than any physical heart could grow.

The power of the unique friendship between a monkey and a crocodile sparked a ripple effect, inspiring a newfound acceptance, understanding, and unity that spread among all the creatures of the jungle. As the sun set over the glistening river, the jungle echoed with sounds of joy and laughter.

Animals, once separated by their differences, now played together, shared stories, and celebrated each other's uniqueness.

Your greatest treasure is your heart's delight,
Unseen by eyes, weightless, and bright.
Cherish it, nurture it, and let it grow,
Its magic sparks an inner-radiant glow.

Chapter 9

Every Crayon Has a Purpose
By Dr. George Garcia

"*Se necesita coraje para tu mija,*" my abuela would always say.

That means it takes courage to be you.

"Wonderfully, beautifully, and uniquely you, *mi amor.*"

Lola was a bright and curious seven-year-old girl. She lived in a small town with friendly neighbors and familiar streets.

She was surrounded by the love and warmth of her abuelos, who lived just a few houses away. Together, they shared many fun days at the park, baking cookies, and out in Abuela's garden.

But one day, everything changed. Lola's dad got a new job in a faraway city, and the family had to pack their belongings and move away from Lola's beloved hometown. Lola was forced to say goodbye to the cookies, adventures in the park, and to her abuela's garden.

As they settled into their new home, Lola found herself facing a world of unfamiliarity. Beginning with the first week of school.

When the first day of school arrived, and Lola, naturally shy, stepped into the bustling hallways as a transfer student, the school was filled with children who seemed to know each other well. Laughter filled the building and echoed throughout the courtyard. As Lola observed her classmates, she couldn't help but notice how out of place she felt. Her curly, brown hair stood out amongst a sea of straight locks, and her vibrant dress, decorated with splashes of colors, sat in contrast with the neutral colors of her peers.

Ms. Peri, Lola's new teacher, ushered the students into the class and began her introductions.

Lola sat quietly at her desk, eyes fixed on the chalkboard, but her mind was a thousand miles away. The classroom buzzed with the sound of pencils scratching against paper and the distant hum of her classmates' whispers. Lola's heart was longing for another place—her abuela's backyard garden.

Slipping into a daydream, Lola was taken back to her abuela's garden, surrounded by the love and warmth she so desperately missed.

Lola could smell the sweet fragrance of Abuela's roses and see the vibrant colors of blooming flowers dancing in the warm breeze. She could feel the soft, warm grass tickling her feet as she ran through the garden, giggling with glee. The memories of Abuela's garden made her feel both happy and deeply homesick.

Lola's mind continued to wander toward an old oak tree that stood near the corner of the garden, next to the nopales cactus. The tree's branches provided shade on hot summer days for Abuela and Lola. A tear welled up in Lola's eye as she imagined picking roses for the dinner table with her abuela and helping prepare the nopales cactus.

As Ms. Peri's voice faded into the background, Lola's daydream became more vivid. She could hear the chirping of birds, the rustling of leaves, and the distant sound of Abuela singing in the backyard. The daydream was both a sweet and sad memory for Lola.

Ring! Ring! Ring!

Lola nearly jumped out of her shoes as the school bell blared over the intercom.

And just like that, the first day of school was over. Having not made a friend, Lola began packing her bag to go home.

Tomorrow will be better, I guess.

Abuela always told me to at least try.

I guess I can try for Abuela.

Ms. Peri, noticing the faint shine of tears on Lola's cheek, walked up to Lola as she collected her backpack.

"Lola, how was your first day?"

Lola, still with tears in her eyes, couldn't muster the words to tell Ms. Peri.

"Moving to a new school is hard, huh?"

Lola shakily nodded.

"You know, when I was your age, I also moved to a new school and a new home. That was really hard for me too. I missed home so much. But my memories always helped me feel close. I realized I could take the feeling of home wherever I went and even share it with others. What's your favorite part about home?"

"Abuela's garden," Lola said softly. "The oak tree, flowers, and nopales cactus."

"Wow," says Ms. Peri, "That sounds wonderful. Well, Lola, you better get to pick-up, but I look forward to hearing more about Abuela's garden."

Lola scurried off to the pick-up line, leaving Ms. Peri with an idea to help bring her students together.

The next morning, Ms. Peri walked to the front of the class, ready to start the first project of the year.

"Okay, class, we're jumping into our first art project. The theme of the assignment is home."

Ms. Peri set down a large box of crayons and began passing out paper.

"I want you all to come up with a picture to tell us a little about your home and what home means to you," explained Ms. Peri.

A soft, steady stream of tears began to flow from Lola's eyes. The directions remind her again of how homesick she felt, but also of the time Ms. Peri spent talking with her about Abuela's garden yesterday.

I can't draw anything.

All I can think about is missing Abuela.

But Abuela said we at least try, so that's what I will do.

"Okay, class, I want you to form a straight line and come pick up to five crayons. The crayons you pick are the crayons you must use for your drawing," Ms. Peri directed.

Lola's classmates all leaped out of their seats and zipped straight to the crayon box. By the time Lola reached the crayon box, all the good colors were seemingly gone.

"I'm going to draw me dunking on my basketball court!" One girl called out.

"Well, I'm going to draw me ziplining to my tree house."

"Double backflips all day on my trampoline."

Everyone seemed so sure of what to draw and so excited to share their memories. They all were so connected to their home.

Lola's knees became weak. Her arms were heavy as she let out a disappointed sigh. Still, without an idea of what to do on the assignment, Lola approached the box.

Sifting through the crayons, Lola's eyes scoured through the box, trying to make the best out of the crayon options left. She glanced over at the corner of the box and noticed a sort of awkward colored green barely popping out amongst the other colors.

"As. . .p. . .ar. . ."

"Asparagus green. Now that is an interesting color," said Ms. Peri with a grin as big as the classroom.

Lola was instantly reminded of her abuela's nopales cactus.

"This is perfect," Lola softly uttered.

Lola grabbed the asparagus green and a few other colors and scurried back to her seat. Bursting with a newfound inspiration, she nearly zipped past her desk in the excitement.

First, the green.

Then, the brown.

Then, light red.

Lola began throwing color all over her sheet. The color began to spill off of her page.

Inspired by its prickly beauty, Lola starts sketching the cactus with great enthusiasm and delight. She carefully drew each tiny spine and every succulent paddle, capturing its unique charm and the warmth of her abuela's garden.

Rrrrrrrrrrrrrring! The school bell blares, bringing the end of the day.

Lola's hands trembled as she walked and stood before her teacher, her heart racing with nervous energy. She took a deep breath, her voice quivering as she made her request.

"Excuse me, Ms. Peri, I have a question."

"Hi Lola, sure. I might have an answer for you."

Smiling, Lola softly presented her request to Ms. Peri. "I was wondering if I could bring my picture to share with the class?" The seconds stretched into eternity until her teacher smiled warmly, encouraging her to proceed.

"What do you mean, Lola?" Ms. Peri asked curiously. "Show me your drawing and tell me about it."

Relief flooded Lola's anxious soul.

"Well, during the hot summer days, abuela and I would pick some of her colorful flowers for the table. She would let me help cut the nopales cactus and pick an apple to eat under the tree.

Home to me is with my abuela. I want to bring some nopalitos and apples to share with the class."

"That's a fantastic idea, Lola."

Lola leaped with joy and sprinted towards the pickup line. When she got home she immediately face-timed her abuela. When her abuela saw the vibrant picture of the nopales cactus, her eyes sparkled with joy as she admired Lola's artwork.

"*Mi amor,* your drawing is beautiful! You captured my garden perfectly," she praised.

Lola, beaming with pride, shared the idea of bringing the nopalitos and apples to class. Then she asked for Abuela's help. Abuela's face lit up with joy.

"Of course, Lola! That would be a wonderful way to share our culture and the beauty of our garden with your class."

Lola's mom called her dad to ask him to pick up some nopales from the grocery store on his way home from work. After what felt like hours, Lola's dad finally arrived home. Lola then excitedly tapped on the FaceTime icon on her momma's phone, connecting with Abuela in her cozy kitchen.

Lola eagerly entered the kitchen and began cooking with her mom and Abuela—the sweet and familiar aroma of simmering apples and the earthy scent of nopalitos filling the air. Lola's mom helped slice the prickly pear cactus pads and remove the thorns.

"It's time to learn the treasured family recipes, *mi amor,*" said Abuela.

Lola hurriedly gathered her ingredients, mirroring Abuela's actions. With encouragement from Abuela and help from her mom, Lola was filled with inspiration.

On the day of the art project presentations, Lola arrived at school with her abuela's delicious nopalitos and sweet apples in hand. As she nervously presented her project, a hush fell over the room, replaced by a collective gasp and awe and admiration.

The classroom curiously buzzed with excitement as Lola shared the story behind her drawing and the snack. Lola painted a picture of Abuela's vibrant garden, the herbs, spices, and, of course, the tall nopales cactus that sits towards the back.

Ms. Peri then passed out the nopalitos and apples to the class.

Ring! Ring! Ring! The school bell signaled recess time.

Among the murmurs and scurrying to get outside, a classmate whom Lola had admired approached her.

"Lola, your drawing is incredible! I've never seen anything like it."

In that instant, a connection sparked between them, like kindred spirits finding solace in shared artistic appreciation. Lola's eyes brimmed with joy as the weight of homesickness began to leave, replaced by a newfound sense of belonging.

Chapter 10

Dusty the Spunky Classroom Bunny
Navigating Grief Together, One Hop at a Time
By Kelly Daugherty

"Dusty has passed away in his sleep."

Miss Miller's eyes filled with tears.

Her voice was shaky as she told us about Dusty's death.

Silence hung heavy in the air.

Greg's eyes began to overflow with tears. "You mean Dusty died?"

Miss Miller nodded, "Yes, Greg. Dusty died and isn't with us anymore."

Cas looked puzzled. "But where did Dusty go?"

Miss Miller knelt down to explain, "When living things die, their bodies stop working. It's a natural part of life."

Tears welled up in Kate's eyes. "So, we won't ever see Dusty again?"

Miss Miller shook her head gently. "We won't see Dusty like before, but we can remember our happy times with him. He lives on in our memories."

Max's brow wrinkled. "But I miss him already."

As the classroom sat there, thinking about Dusty and missing him, Greg's mind thought back to a cool September morning and that special day when they first met Dusty.

Greg, a boy with sandy-brown hair wearing his favorite video game t-shirt, lined up outside his new classroom, along with Eileen, Max, Cas, and all the other kids of his 4th grade class, waiting to go inside.

Greg was so impatient that he couldn't stand still; he bounced around like a rubber ball, "Are you excited, Eileen?" His voice was full of happiness and curiosity, just like a kid looking forward to an exciting adventure.

Eileen, a girl with long brown hair and the friendliest smile wearing a purple princess t-shirt, nodded excitedly, "Yeah! I wonder what our new classroom looks like?"

Kate, a girl with bright blue eyes that glittered with a touch of mischief, stood there, looking lovely in her new sparkly pink dress that matched the twinkle in her eyes. "I heard Miss Miller is really nice," Kate said.

With wide, curious eyes, Kiera examined her new pencil case, a delightful sky-blue shade decorated with colorful bunnies that pranced among fluffy clouds. Kiera gently ran her fingers over the soft fabric, feeling the bunny's whimsical design. "I wonder who I will sit next to?"

The classroom door swung open, and their eager steps carried them inside.

The room was a colorful, safe place. What captured their attention was a cage decorated with ribbons, inside of which sat Dusty, a fluffy brown bunny with fur as soft as velvet.

"Look! It's Dusty!" Greg shouted, running to the cage as fast as his legs could carry him. He remembered seeing Dusty last year when he visited the classroom with his older brother. The other kids followed quickly, their laughter filling the air, excited to meet the bunny Greg had told them about.

Miss Miller beamed with a kind and welcoming smile. "Yes, this is Dusty, our special classroom bunny. Friends, come sit on the rug and let me introduce you to our furry friend."

The students huddled closely on the cozy rug, their eyes bright with enthusiasm and curiosity, all set to meet Dusty.

Miss Miller continued, her voice warm and gentle. "Dusty is incredibly sweet and holds a very special place in our classroom. Each of you will play an important role in caring for Dusty."

Miss Miller then handed out special jobs, like candy, to the students.

"Alek, you will be in charge of feeding Dusty every morning before class starts. You'll make sure he has his breakfast and fresh hay."

"Eileen," she said with a smile, "you'll be responsible for cleaning Dusty's litter box. It's important to keep it tidy."

Turning to Kate, Miss Miller said, "Kate, you can give Dusty some tasty treats during our reading time. But remember, just a few treats so he doesn't overeat!"

"And Kiera," she added, "you'll make sure Dusty always has fresh water. We want him to stay hydrated."

The students nodded eagerly, thrilled to have their very own responsibilities when it came time to take care of Dusty. This sweet bunny had already brought joy to their classroom, and now they were determined to ensure he felt loved and cared for every day.

As they cared for him together, they learned about responsibility and teamwork. Taking turns feeding Dusty and cleaning his cage brought them closer, and they realized that working together made everything easier.

Dusty wasn't just a bunny; he was like a friend who made school days happier.

They laughed at his funny hops and giggled as he nibbled on carrots.

They loved being around him, telling stories, sharing secrets, and felt comforted by him. Even when things were tough, Dusty could always make them smile. Sometimes, he would playfully flop over on his side after a big hop, or he would come up close and gently bump his nose with their hands, asking for a pet. His soft fur was like a warm hug that made them feel better during schoolwork and tests. Dusty's playful and loving actions always brightened their day.

Dusty had a special way of making normal school moments super fun, like when he hopped onto a student's desk during math class, and everyone couldn't stop laughing. Or when he snuggled up to someone reading a book, making them feel all cozy inside. Their friendship with Dusty was super special, like having a happy, fluffy buddy in the classroom with them.

Weeks turned into months, and Dusty became the heart of the classroom.

Dusty's magic didn't stop there. Dusty also showed them how to be kind and caring. One day, when Greg felt sad because he forgot his lunch, Dusty quietly hopped over and sat beside him. Greg gently petted Dusty, and his tears started to go away. Seeing how much Dusty cheered Greg up, his friend Cas decided to share his sandwich with Greg, and Kiera gave him some of her apple.

When Dusty sat with Greg when he was upset, he helped everyone see the importance of being there for friends and understanding each other's feelings. This made everyone in the class care more about each other, like a close-knit family.

One day, when Eileen felt nervous about a big presentation, Dusty hopped over and nuzzled her hand. It was as if he knew she needed encouragement. The other students gathered around, offering words of support and friendship. With Dusty's comforting presence and the support of her classmates, Eileen gave a fantastic presentation that earned her a round of applause.

As they navigated the ups and downs of school life, Dusty became a symbol of their friendship. They looked out for each other like they looked out for Dusty. They shared happy moments and their worries and fears, knowing that together, they could face anything.

Greg blinked and returned to the present, listening to Miss Miller's gentle voice as she shared the sad news about Dusty.

Miss Miller's voice was soft and kind, like a warm blanket. "It's okay to miss Dusty. He was a special friend. It's okay to feel sad," she said softly. "We can share our feelings and remember Dusty in our own ways."

Their classroom became a safe space for sharing feelings. Tears flowed freely, proof of their love and grief. They remembered Dusty's joyful hops and how his fur felt soft under their touch.

"I remember when Dusty hopped like a kangaroo," Greg grinned, his eyes bright with the memory.

Eileen added, "And how he would nudge our hands for more carrots or when he knew we were sad," she whispered as a tear ran down her cheek.

Cas sniffled. "I liked giving Dusty carrots. He was so gentle."

Max looked thoughtful, "I remember how Dusty's fur felt when I petted him. It was like touching a cloud."

Kate smiled through her tears. "Dusty was our friend, and we'll never forget him."

Miss Miller nodded. "Exactly. Even though Dusty isn't here anymore, we have all these wonderful memories."

With Miss Miller's help, they decided to create a special memorial for Dusty. They carefully cleaned his cage one last time, a mix of responsibility and love. Armed with crayons, markers, and paper, they poured their emotions onto pages to create pictures of Dusty.

Greg drew Dusty mid-hop, capturing his energy. Eileen's artwork showed Dusty's curious look, reflecting their own wonder. Alek's drawing showed Dusty munching on a giant carrot.

As they attached their drawings to Dusty's cage, the room felt both sad and warm. "We'll always remember you, Dusty," Kiera whispered, her voice a soft promise.

Miss Miller smiled at their artwork. "This is a beautiful way to honor Dusty's memory. He'll always have a place in our hearts."

Their drawings converted Dusty's cage into a vibrant collage of love and memories. The room buzzed with emotions, sadness, and gratitude for the memories they shared and the love Dusty gave them.

As they looked at Dusty's cage, covered in their colorful drawings, they knew their special friend would always be a part of their hearts, guiding them through their journey of life.

They gathered around Dusty's cage; Miss Miller spoke softly, "Dusty taught us many things. He taught us about joy, responsibility, and even about saying goodbye. But most importantly, he taught us that even though things change, the love and connection we share remains."

Tears welled up in their eyes as they looked at Dusty's cage. Greg's voice shook as he shared, "Dusty showed us how to be happy, even when things are sad. And he brought us all together, making us better friends."

Miss Miller's words were like a cozy Dusty bunny hug, "Life is like a big book with many parts. Dusty was one of those parts, and it was full of joy, fun, sometimes sadness, and tears. Let's remember the bond of friendship and the things Dusty taught us; they will always show us the way."

The class chose to make a little garden outside their school. It had lots of colorful flowers, and they made a special part just for Dusty, their bunny. As the kids from Miss Miller's class grew up, they would often go back to visit her and then walk by the garden. They would stop and think about Dusty, their bunny friend, and all the good times they had. They remembered the important things they learned about grief, making friends, and being kind. They believed that Dusty's spirit would stay with them, helping them remember the good times and love they had together in Miss Miller's class.

Chapter 11

You Are Magic
By Indya J. Clark

"Good morning, class," began second-grade teacher Mrs. Soul. "I hope you all had a great weekend! We will start our day by covering all the exciting things planned for our week."

Joi sat up excitedly at her table with her friends Amirah and Royalty in their assigned seats.

Every Monday morning, Mrs. Soul would greet the class, assign new jobs to her students for the week, and talk about Share Out Time.

Share Out Time was when one lucky second grader got to stand up in front of the class and tell the class about one special item, and afterward, the entire class got to eat delicious food and treats they'd brought.

Joi had yet to get chosen. Today, she was gleaming because today felt like the day. Joi closed her eyes and sat in her chair smiling, imagining it was her turn for Share Out Time.

With her eyes closed, Joi imagined Mrs. Soul reaching into the hat full of student's names. She imagined her hand pulling out a piece of paper with her name on it.

The next thing Joi heard was. . .

"And last but not least," said Mrs. Soul, "our Share Out leader of the week is—drumroll please, class—Joi Clarkson!"

Joi's friends high-fived her across the table.

"Joi, we cannot wait to have you lead our Share Out Time this week!" said Mrs. Soul, "So, remember, you get to lead the class tomorrow and share something very special to you."

"I'll remember, and I'll be ready!" claimed Joi.

"I can't believe it's your turn!" exclaimed Royalty.

"Oh my gosh, I know," Joi said.

"Are you nervous?" asked Amirah.

"Nervous? What do you mean, nervous?" said Joi.

"Well, you'll have to talk in front of the whole class and share something special! That's a big deal. Everyone will be looking at *you*."

Joi stopped. "I didn't think about that part."

Before today, all Joi could think about was having her turn to share something special, unique, or extraordinary. It never ever crossed her mind what it'd be like to speak in front of the class.

Jois's excitement turned to worry. She had difficulty enjoying her favorite classes for the rest of the day and didn't enjoy finishing her painting her best friend—a stuffed animal named King, in art class. She didn't gobble down her favorite dessert at lunchtime, the strawberry shortcake, and didn't even enjoy the movie day they had in dance class since there was a substitute.

All Joi could think about was Share Out Day and how nervous she was.

Would I forget my words?

Would I be all sweaty and stinky when I stand up in front of the class?

What should I talk about?

What if this happened, or that?

Maybe I was not so lucky to be the next to share at Share Out Time.

When the school bell rang, the students at Jerold Eugene Elementary gathered their things in a hurry to go home. Joi was the last to leave the classroom.

"See you tomorrow, Joi! I can't wait to see what you'll share with us," shouted Mrs. Soul as Joi exited.

Joi didn't reply. She was now very nervous about Share Out Time.

Joi walked down the school entryway and saw her mom and sister, Reign, waving from the car.

"Hey, girl!" Joi's mom excitedly greeted as Joi got into the backseat. "Why the long face? Wasn't today the day you discovered whose turn it was for Share Out Time?"

Sigh. Joi's shoulders dropped.

"Yeah, it was," said Joi as she propped her head on the window, gazing as the trees went by.

Joi's mom and sister looked at each other, confused.

"Well?" said mom and Reign at the same time.

"It's my turn to share out tomorrow," Joi said.

Joi's mom and big sister Reign smiled and did their famous happy dance. They raised their arms and wiggled their hips in excitement. Suddenly, they both stopped when they noticed Joi was not celebrating with them.

"I'm so nervous, and now I don't know if I can stand up in front of the class tomorrow and share after all," said Joi as she squirmed in her chair and clenched her backpack.

The car went quiet.

Silence.

This was a side of Joi no one had seen before.

As Joi's mom drove up in front of their cozy home, Joi's mom and sister both reached back to hold one of her hands.

Joi took a deep breath and walked from the car to her bedroom. Her legs felt heavy, and her head felt like a balloon that just wanted to float away.

Joi slipped her backpack across the bedroom, ran, and jumped onto her bed. When her head touched her pillow, she closed her eyes, trying to go to her happy place within her mind. She spread her arms out, and at her fingertips, she could feel her favorite stuffed animal, King.

King was very special to her. He was her black and brown stuffed animal dog toy which she had ever since she was born.

King made her feel safe.

King made her feel strong.

King made her feel brave.

It was King who reminded her that everything would be okay, especially on new and exciting but also scary adventures, whether in her imaginary adventures or at school.

King also had a little bit of magic inside him—as Reign, her sister, would always remind her he could talk, but only to Joi.

Just as Joi was about to reach out for King, Joi heard a knock at the door.

"Who is it?" Joi shouted.

"It's me Reign. Can I come in?"

"Yes," Joi replied.

"Hey, girl," said Reign as she hopped on the bed to sit next to Joi.

Joi gave her a soft smile.

"I just wanted to see how you're doing. Still nervous?" Reign asked.

"Yes. After talking to my friends, I didn't realize how scary talking in front of my class could be."

"Ahhhh," said Reign. "Doing something new can be scary, but you forgot something."

Joi sat there confused, *What is Reign talking about? What did I forget?*

Reign continued, "Joi, you forgot that *you are magic*! See, when you are magic, you can put your mind to anything and do it. When you are magic like you are, you can be anything and still be amazing. You can be happy, sad, nervous, or glad. No matter what you're feeling.

Reign stopped and gave Joi a big smile. "Remember, it's okay to feel however you feel because *you are magic*. And when *you're* magic, *you* can do anything!"

"Thanks, Reign," said Joi. "You're the best sister."

"You've got this, Joi! Do me one more favor before you consider what you'll bring to Share Out Time: talk to King. He always seems to give you an extra sprinkle of courage."

Joi fell into her sister's arms and gave her a big hug!

"I gotta go help Mom with dinner. I'll catch up with you later," said Reign.

Joi started to feel much better. She grabbed King by the paw and closed her eyes. When she closed her eyes, King came to life in her imagination as they began feeling free and danced all around her bedroom.

King hugged Joi and said, "No high-five or smile today? What's wrong, Joi?"

"I'm sorry I'm late, King. Guess what? Tomorrow is my turn to share at Share Out Time," replied Joi

"Yay! I know you're going to do great," said King.

"That's what everyone keeps saying, but I've been nervous all day."

"Do you know how I know you can do it and will be great at it? Because you've stood up for your friend when somebody teased her at school, sang your first song at the school recital, and tried the giant slide at the Waterpark even though it gave you the heebie-jeebies. You're one of the *bravest* people I know."

"King!" Joi happily shouted. "You're right. I did do all of those things!"

King laughed, "Yes, you did, Joi!"

"You've always been my best buddy and cheerleader. I have an idea. Would you mind if I brought you to Share Out Time?" said Joi.

King did a cartwheel. "Wooohoooooooo! What am I going to wear, Joy? What will you wear?"

That night after dinner, as Joi picked out King's outfit for Share Out Time, she imagined she and King were on a shopping spree, trying out every outfit she could dream up—a clown suit and a soccer uniform.

Among all the options, she thought up the perfect outfit for King and herself! None at all—because he was great just as he was.

The next day, Joi rode in the car on the way to school feeling great and wearing her favorite superhero t-shirt and jeans. While King was dressed in just his smile.

"Hey Joi! Are you ready for today?" said Amirah when Joi got out of the car.

"Now I am," said Joi as she raced Amirah to her second-grade classroom and hung up her backpack.

Joi had a whole new feeling today. Today, she knew **she was magic.**

As the class gathered for Share Out Time, Mrs. Soul ensured all the tasty snacks were ready for afterward.

Joi beamed as she took it all in. Everyone was here to hear what she had to say and share.

"Okay, class, it's time to come to the circle for Share Out Time," said Mrs. Soul.

Everyone cheered!

"Joi, do you have your special Share Out Time item for us," asked Mrs. Soul.

Joi ran over to her backpack and took out King. No costume, just him because he was great no matter what he was feeling or wearing. King was her best friend and partner.

King made her feel safe.

King made her feel strong.

King made her feel brave.

King reminded her that she'd be okay.

Joi hugged King. As he hugged her back, King whispered, "It's showtime, Joi. You can do it, and you are going to be great."

Joi gave him the biggest smile.

"Alright, Joi. What do you have to share with us today?" asked Mrs. Soul.

Joi looked at the crowd, took a deep breath, smiled, and began.

"Hi everyone. I'm sharing with you a special friend of mine. This is King. King goes with me on all my adventures. He makes me feel safe; he makes me feel strong and okay. Most of all, he reminds me that I am magic and I can do brave things."

danaus plexippus

Chapter 12

Superpowers
By Rose Aehle

"Oh boy," Oscar muttered, "I'm in a situation!"

Oscar stopped and corrected himself. "Hold on—that's not the right word. . ."

Oscar *was* in a bit of a mess, but for Oscar, it was *most* important to use just the right word to describe this current challenge. After all, this was his superpower, using BIG WORDS like:

". . .Quandary, that's it! I am in a *quandary*."

After Oscar congratulated himself for using just the right term, he turned his attention to the current *quandary* in which he found himself.

He was high up in a tree he had not climbed!

How did he get there?

He had flown to the top of the tree and could barely believe it!

Before finding himself high in the tree, Oscar had been on the ground playing in the park, thinking of big words that were better than the word *incredible.*

Words like:
Spectacular
Stupendous
Astonishing

To his surprise, as he thought of each word, his feet began to float off the ground, and then, to his *astonishment,* he began to fly.

As Oscar flew up into the air alongside an orange, black, and white butterfly; he remembered a better word for the word butterfly,

Rhopalocera!
But not just any Rhopalocera, he thought.
A Danaus plexippus.

These words made him soar even higher and then into the tree he was currently in.

As he contemplated his situation, Oscar heard his mom calling for him,

"OSCAR!" WHERE ARE YOU?" his mom hollered, looking frantically around, not knowing Oscar was high above her head almost at the top of a tall evergreen tree.

This is not going to go well, Oscar thought.

Oscar took a deep breath, "I'm here, Mom! Look up!"

Oscar's mom looked up a bit, then higher, until she saw her son way up in a tree, almost at the tree's tip.

She let out a horrific scream!

"Oscar! How. . .oh my. . .what in the world? Where is my phone? Don't move!"

"Mom! I flew up here!"

"Oscar, do not lie! This is too serious!"

"This is not a *fabrication* of the truth, Mom!" he hollered back, "I did fly up here. Watch me!"

Oscar stepped out into the air; his choice of the word *fabrication* allowed him to gently float down to the ground, landing in front of his terrified mom.

"Oscar! Are you hurt? What is going on?!"

Oscar's poor mom couldn't believe what she had just seen.

"Mom, now please listen." Oscar took a deep breath. "I was contemplating *sesquipedalian* terms like *Rhopalocera,* and *spectacular,* and with each word, I began to *aviate.*"

Oscar's mom took a deep breath. "Oscar, this is *not* the time to use your big words. Just tell me what happened."

Oscar looked puzzled. He thought he had explained the situation perfectly. "I was thinking of big words for 'butterfly' and 'awesome', and with each big word, I started to float, and then I began to fly."

Oscar's mom looked at Oscar, disbelieving. "I don't understand?"

"Just watch!"

Oscar said the word *quandary* and his feet began to float off the ground. Then he said the word *aviate* and began to fly.

"Oscar, come back down now, please."

His mom looked upset. First, her son was confusing everyone, including his teachers, with his use of large words, and now this. It was too much!

But Oscar was delighted.

I am ecstatic. He thought. *I have two superpowers now! I am going to use them every day!*

His parents tried to reason with Oscar, telling him that using big words to fly was not a good idea to do constantly, but it was not that easy. Oscar's feet would float up every time he said or thought large words. His parents also explained that while flying was unique not everyone would want to hear his big words all the time, especially just so he could fly.

But Oscar didn't listen. He was too excited. He had to show the world his two superpowers.

Soon, Oscar became known as the flying boy who would soar and dip over everyone's heads, shouting out words like:

Rudimentary!
Finesse!
Aspiration!
Bulbous!

His friends began to find this annoying. But Oscar didn't care. He loved showing off his two superpowers.

However, just like his parents had warned him, the other kids got tired of Oscar's flying and shouting out big words, so they stopped wanting to play with him.

He also became the main target of Jim, the class bully. Jim was the boy who was always pushing others, coughing in people's faces, and picking on any kid who crossed his path.

Jim really didn't like Oscar because once Oscar had called him *Phlegm Jim* after Jim had coughed up some gunk and spat it out on the ground. Oscar's mom had told Oscar that calling Jim that name was not very nice, but Oscar thought he was being very clever. Nevertheless, with Oscar's flying and yelling out big words, Jim got meaner because of Oscar's teasing.

"You're a stupid bird who says stupid words," Jim would mock as he flapped his arms like a bird.

Jim not only made fun of Oscar, but he also pushed him whenever he could to see if he could make Oscar fly into the walls. The other kids, including his friends, didn't even help Oscar when this happened.

This made Oscar feel very alone and very sad. He was also confused.

I have two superpowers that no one else has.

No one wants to play with me.

Oscar stopped saying large words, and so the flying also stopped. While this seemed to keep Jim from bothering him, Oscar felt unhappy.

I am sad. Oscar thought. *No one likes me or my superpowers.*

When Jim suddenly stopped coming to school, Oscar still did not use any large words with his friends, which meant he also stopped flying in front of them. He would just use big words to float when no one was around. But when Jim continued to stay out of school, curiosity got the best of Oscar.

"Mom, Jim isn't in school anymore. Did he move?" Oscar asked his mom one day.

Oscar's mom shook her head. "Jim is in the hospital with a very serious disease that is affecting his lungs."

What? Oscar's eyes opened wide.

"He's in a room where people who visit him have to wear very special clothes before they go in the room so they don't make him sicker."

"You mean he's in *reverse isolation?*" Oscar asked.

Oscar's mom looked surprised.

"That sounds right. How did you know those words?"

Oscar sighed, "I was bored and started looking at a medical dictionary for bigger words."

Then he added to himself, *and learning big words lets me float around.*

"He can't have visitors, can he, Mom?" Oscar asked.

His mom shook her head.

"Not really; only his parents can visit him."

Oscar went silent. He didn't like Jim. Jim had made fun of him and been mean to him. But Jim was sick, and whatever was making Jim sick sounded serious, and now Jim was alone in the hospital most of the time.

If I was in a hospital all alone, I would be very frightened and sad. And with that thought, Oscar, even though he felt scared, decided maybe this might be the right time to use his superpowers to help Jim. After all, Jim couldn't chase him if he was in a hospital, but maybe flying over to see him might make him feel less lonely.

"Mom, can I fly up to Jim's window at the hospital and see him?"

Oscar's mom looked at her son thoughtfully. This was a brave thing he was asking to do. She knew how he had struggled over the last few days. She knew he had misused his superpowers to the point that his friends did not want to be with him. But this might be a good way for Oscar to use his love of words that made him fly.

Oscar's mom agreed, and after clearing the idea with the hospital, where everyone had heard of Oscar and his flying, Oscar was allowed to surprise Jim with a flying visit.

"I can fly up and hold a note that says, **I wish you a positive** *prognosis*!" Oscar said excitedly.

His mom smiled and suggested.

"Maybe it might be better just to write **Get Better Soon.**"

Oscar agreed.

"But I have to at least *think* of big words so I can fly up to see Jim."

On the day of the hospital visit, Oscar, under the watchful eyes of his mom, began to fly up to the fifth-floor window where Jim was sitting sadly in his bed with an oxygen mask on his face.

When Oscar got to the window, he tapped.

Jim turned and saw Oscar, nose squished against the glass, holding a paper close to the window that read **Get Well Soon!**

Jim giggled; his eyes lit up.

He sat up, clapped, and waved.

Oscar was so happy at this reaction that he somersaulted in the air.

He dipped down and brought up another paper, this one did have the big words Oscar had wanted to write.

I wish you a positive *prognosis*!

Jim looked puzzled for a minute as he read the word *prog-no-sis*.

Jim then realized that this second sign meant the same thing as the first sign Oscar had held up. As soon as Jim figured this out, he began to float!

Oscar was shocked when he saw Jim floating, and at first, he was worried that this might hurt Jim, but Jim was smiling!

Oscar flew to the hospital daily, holding up different signs with big words, and Jim would look the words up in his online dictionary. Each time Jim discovered and understood the meaning of the words, he would float in his hospital room with Oscar flying outside the window looking in.

When Jim came back to school, Jim and Oscar began sharing their love of words with their friends. Soon, their friends began flying with Jim and Oscar, as they enjoyed this superpower of learning new words.

"This is super!" Oscar shouted.

And Jim and his other friends smiled and shouted back.

"Superlative!"

"Exceptional!"

And off they all flew, enjoying their words.

Chapter 13

Dear Diary
Rosa, I'm coming home!
By Lorie Weed

Dear Diary,

Thursday

Today is the worst day of my life!

My best friend is gone! We can't find her!

She has never left the front yard before, even with the gate open. My dad said he never really had to train her. She was so smart; she *knew* the right things to do.

My mom gave me this book to help me feel better. She said writing down our sad feelings helps us work through our emotions and can help us to understand ourselves. On the cover is a picture of a dog that looks just like Liam. Fuzzy golden brown and black fur. Pointy ears straight up. A black wet nose and a smile with light in her eyes. That's how Liam looked when I'd talk to her every day.

My name is Rosa. If it's okay, I'll just call you Diary, like it says on the cover. It also says 'journal,' but I like Diary better.

I'm just so sad and worried for Liam!

I should tell you what happened.

When I got home from school today, my mom asked, "Did you see Liam this morning?" Of course, I saw Liam! She sleeps with me every night. She spends her days out in the yard. As my dad says, she is doing her job guarding. When I left for school, she walked me to the gate.

That's when I realized she didn't greet me at the gate when I got home.

My mom said the gate was wide open when she got home from work, and Liam was nowhere to be seen.

I ran back outside and looked in all our favorite spots— under the lilac tree, the playhouse by the swing, and our mud puddle spot. I called her name, but nothing. Even the wind chimes on the maple tree were silent.

I checked inside the dog house. Sometimes, we would hide in there—still no Liam.

Liam: Where are they taking me?

Friday

I couldn't sleep last night. Liam's soft fur and warm body were missing beside me. Usually, she takes up most of the bed and steals all the blankets.

Today, my mom and dad let me stay home from school so I could help look for Liam. We walked around the neighborhood and called her name a lot. We asked Mrs. Marino, our neighbor who stays home to watch her grandchildren if she had seen Liam. She thought she heard a dog barking but didn't look out her window to see who it might be.

Mom called the humane society. That's where animals without homes go. Mom said lost animals sometimes get taken there if somebody finds them. The lady on the phone had a good idea. She said to put Liam's bed outside to help her smell her way home. Mom said a blanket would do since we share my twin bed. We have always shared everything.

I put our favorite blanket, the one with the pink hearts, under the lilacs. The blanket is our favorite because it's the softest.

Liam: Where are they taking me?
What are they putting on my face?

Monday

It's been a couple of days since I last wrote here. I miss Liam so much. I don't know why she left. I wonder if I did something to make her mad. I wish I could tell her I'm sorry. I've been sleeping with a stuffed Liam my Lito and Lita gave me. That's my grandparents. They miss her, too.

When I was one year old, Liam was just a puppy. I wouldn't fall asleep if I couldn't see Liam from my crib. I cried until Mom and Dad brought her near me. Mom said that's how Liam earned her way to sleep in my room. Otherwise, she would have been outside all the time, sleeping in her dog house at night. I'm glad my dad changed his mind.

I hope Liam has a warm place to sleep tonight.

> *Liam: The smells here are nothing like home.*
> *I can feel Rosa being so sad. I need to get home to her.*
> *They finally stopped driving.*

Tuesday

My dad told me today that Liam might never come back! He had tears in his eyes. I could tell he was trying not to cry. Dad said he wouldn't stop looking. I know I'll never stop looking. I can't imagine my life without her. Even if she stays mad at me, I want her to come home.

Wednesday

At school today, my class helped make lost dog posters. Everyone worked hard on them. Most of my classmates have met Liam from sleepovers or just walking past the house. Liam always reached over the gate to say hello and give sloppy kisses.

My teacher, Ms. Amery, the best second-grade teacher ever, said she would put the posters up right after school today.

I hope someone recognizes her and helps her come home.

I miss you, Liam.

Liam: All these dogs.
Why do they want us to fight?
These are not good men.
I must find a way out.
I need to get back to my family.
Rosa, I'm coming home.

Friday

I woke up from a terrible dream.

I had just climbed into bed when I saw Liam with my mind's eye. She had blood on her face! She was hurt! Her eyes looked so sad. I told my mom and dad about it and said we had to find her. They held me and told me not to think about it. It was just a bad dream, they said.

Liam: I've been watching these men closely.
One of them doesn't close the doors tight when he throws food in
the cages. I will make my escape the next time he feeds us.
Rosa, I'm coming home.

Monday

Before I woke up this morning, I heard Liam say she was coming home!

I could see her looking into my eyes. I told Mom and Dad. They looked sadder than ever. My dad told me he had talked to Mr. Garcia, our neighbor next door. Mr. Garcia saw two men looking at the lamppost in front of our house. At first, he thought they were workers from the city, but after hearing about Liam missing and still not found, Mr. Garcia fears she was taken for the dog fights.

Taken?!

Dog fight?!

That's why her face was bleeding! She must be okay! Right Diary? I mean, didn't I hear her say she was coming home?

> *Liam: These men are getting excited about something.*
> *I can't tell why, but I'm sure it isn't for anything good.*
> *They brought another dog in. Much smaller than me.*
> *I'm a petite German Shepherd. As I've heard the veterinarian say.*
> *The new dog is the size of a football, with curly fur and floppy ears.*
> *He'd never survive a fight.*

Thursday

Today, my parents took me to the pet store. On the front door, was one of the posters my class made. Only now, it looks so worn and faded. My heart ached. Liam has been gone a long time. They wanted to surprise me with a new puppy. I told them I didn't want a new puppy. I'm waiting for Liam to come home.

Liam: There were so many men here today.
I was starting to worry if I could ever be able to escape this cage.
Then, a miracle happened.
Some of the men began to fight themselves.
One of them fell right on top of my cage!
The door latch came open. No one noticed.
Rosa, I'm coming home.

Friday

So many things remind me of Liam. I see her everywhere. The fur that's on my clothes, the shoe she chewed my laces on. Every time I look at the swing set. Seeing a dog on TV do the same tricks. I remember the mud pies we made together after the storm passed. I miss her. I hope I didn't dream of her saying she's coming home.

Liam: It was dark and quiet.
The rusty cage door opened with a squeak.
I held still, listening—no sound of humans.
I'm free! I checked the other cages. Those, too, were barely closed.
No one checked the cages. All of us dogs are cold and hungry.
Some of them went their own way. Some came with me.
Rosa, I'm coming home!

Saturday

Something woke me up. It's super early in the morning. Mom and Dad are still sleeping. I can hear Dad snore. The house is scary at night without Liam with me. Especially when the wind sounds so creepy finding the cracks in the walls. It's getting colder outside, and the leaves on the trees are starting to turn colors. Liam and I always looked forward to jumping in the leaf piles and making them crunch. It was so much fun. I think I'll skip the leaves this year.

I keep seeing her in my mind's eye. My teacher, Ms. Amery, said that maybe I was picking up Liam thinking about me, that, sometimes, when great love is shared, souls connect even when there is distance between them. I hope that's true.

> *Liam: We've been walking since we left that awful place.*
> *We met a few local strays who helped point out our way home.*
> *They wanted us to join them, but I told them I was going home to Rosa.*
> *They knew who she was! She always feeds the strays.*
> *She has a really big heart.*

Monday

Today was the best day ever!

When I got home, I walked through the gate, and there she was! She was lying on our favorite pink heart blanket! As soon as we locked eyes, we ran to each other. I have never been so happy! She had brought a few new friends with her. They all looked cold and hurt in some way. Liam's face has wounds all over. Some of them are already healed. My dad let me bring all of the dogs inside. We fed them, bathed them and I made a special bed for each one. My mom is going to check and see if anyone is looking for these dogs. Dad said they can stay as long as they need to.

Of course, Liam is back in the twin bed with me.

From now on, Liam will be guarding from inside the house when no one is home.

Thank you, Diary, for listening to me when Liam was gone. You helped me with my bad dreams, and you knew what I meant about hearing Liam say she was coming home. I'll never forget that, or you.

Your friend forever.

Love, Rosa

Chapter 14

Emmy the Dragon Finds a Fallen Star

By Atlantis Wolf

T*HAR-RA-RAH-KAH-THOOOOM!*

A smashing sound on planet Hozho sent quake waves through oceans, mountains, and polar ice caps.

Emmy was sleeping in her cave with her massive head sticking out beside the Oyo River.

Her red scales and bronze horns were being warmed by the first rays of morning sunlight. When a thunderous boom arrived, she yawned and rolled her head to one side. The lustrous gold scales under her chin absorbed the sun's warmth.

She opened one of her sapphire-blue eyes.

Did I hear something? she thought. *No, no. Not now. Not at my favorite time of the day. Not likely.*

She fell back asleep.

Emmy was a fire dragon. She loved making fires and watching fires. Every night, she fell asleep smiling as she watched millions of star-fires flicker in the night sky.

Every morning, she loved feeling her planet's star-fire, Shay, waking her with his nourishing rays of golden light. She loved the way he gradually bathed her face and shoulders, coaxing her to inch out of her cave and sun herself.

But today was different.

A swarm of fairies from Adohee Forest came buzzing through the air, heading for Emmy. A gaggle of gnomes came bolting out of their deep burrows and dens around her cave, rushing up to her on three sides. And Yuki, the rainbow-maned unicorn, came galloping toward her from Zander Mountain across the river.

"Emmy, Emmy, Emmy!" they shouted. "Wake up, wake up, wake up!"

Too late.

A quake wave had traveled around the planet. Oyo's normally flat surface was propelled into a tidal wave that crashed over Emmy's head, wings, and tail, filling her cave with water.

"YEE-AAHHRH-AGGGPAHAAA!"

Emmy roared as she tumbled against the cave walls along with over a hundred gnomes. She stomped out of the cave, gnomes dangling from her scales and horns; a few circled around her legs as the wave of water subsided. She set them down in the field of white Xixian flowers and fished one remaining gnome out of the river.

Then Emmy lifted her head toward the sky and spread her red feathered wings as wide as the horizon. She closed her eyes. Her scales started glowing like embers. The water on them hissed and boiled, creating a cloud of steam around her. With a final flap of her wings and rippling shake of her skin, she was dry.

"Yuki, what happened?"

"A giant ball of white light fell from the sky and then disappeared."

"I'll have a look," said Emmy as she crouched and launched skyward. "Gnome nation, please see about drying my cave. Fairy friends, please find my treasures, scrolls, and crystals. I'll be back."

Emmy was a planet guardian. She spent every day protecting and caring for Hozho. She had a relationship with all four-legged animals, winged ones, and sea creatures. Even trees, insects, and clouds. She treated everyone as relatives, as family.

Emmy flew over Zander Mountain. She saw a streak of black charred ground leading to a circular crater. As she swooped down into the steaming, hot dirt and burned trees, she saw the crater was empty. It was like looking at a place where a big fireball had dropped, crashed through trees and rocks, and rolled to a stop. But there was nothing left.

Emmy landed and walked on scorched, crunchy rubble with her black feet and iron claws. Everywhere she stepped was charred earth, sooty and ashen. And noiseless. Only the sound of burning wood and cracking earth were in her ears. She walked to the center of the scoop, the middle of the crater.

Woof! This is going to be a big project, she thought. Gnomes can smooth the land. Fairies can start planting flowers and ivy. Yuki and I can draw a map of where to replant the trees.

Emmy surveyed, walking and thinking. Then she heard a sound, a tiny sound like trickling water over a stone or a child's body curling into a ball when they're sad.

She looked and saw nothing. She listened again.

She walked to the edge, put her snout to the ground, and inhaled all the air. Curious, she used one claw to turn over a blackened rock. There it was—a pearl of dazzling white, luminous light, a speck of twinkle-light.

Why is it so small? she thought, rolling it into her hand. Tiny shards of white light fell off as it rolled across her huge palm.

"Oh no!" she said. "What's the matter, Bubby?"

"I don't know what to do," said Twinkle-Speck. "I was feeling small and scared and lonely and cold. I fell. And now, I just want my light to go out."

Emmy was quiet and said, "I see. Would you like to come sit with me?"

"Sure."

Emmy closed her warm hand around Speck and flew back to her cave.

"Friends," said Emmy as she landed. "I have a surprise." She opened her clawed hand as they surrounded her.

"Twinkle-light!" they all said.

"Our friend is cold and needs a listening fire."

Gnomes arranged stones in a circle on the beach. Yuki asked forest trees for firewood. Fairies gathered sage, sweetgrass, and pinecones. Emmy arranged it all with one hand while holding Twinkle-Speck in the other—pinecone cluster first, then tinder, sage, kindling, sticks, and sweetgrass to form a pyramid.

Emmy closed her eyes, extending one claw toward the waiting wood pile. A single lick of flame appeared at her clawtip. She lit the pinecones. The fire reached up like slender fingers feeling each flammable component. She added smaller tree branches, then bigger ones. The fire filled the circle with invisible waves of heat and radiant, pulsing light.

As Speck became warmer, he grew in size, filling her whole open hand. The wood branches transformed into dancing and crackling fire sprites with trails of sparks in their smoke hair. Mesmerized, they all gazed at the sky-bound dancers in a long hush of silence.

Speck spoke.

"My mom won't let me be myself. She tells me I'm pink light, but I'm only pink on the outside. Inside, I'm blue."

Emmy, gnomes, fairies, and Yuki turned and peered closer at the translucent, twinkle-light ball. It was iridescent white in the center, with ribbons and rays of blue. The outside shell was shimmering pink orbs.

"You are as you say," said Emmy. "And resplendent. I've never seen a lovelier combination."

Everyone nodded.

"Speck, where is your mother?"

"Far away. She was drinking potion bottles and got really angry when I said I wanted to change my name to a blue name. She said she gave me a pink name when I was born, and that was my name forever."

"Is she human?" asked Emmy.

"Uh-huh."

"Well, no humans live here. You can give yourself any name."

Twinkle-Speck popped into a mammoth-sized ball. "Really?"

Emmy looked at the expanding ball of glittering light and put it down next to her.

"Do you know what you are?"

"No. My mom said she would tell me someday."

"No one can tell you who you are. You blossom into being. Like a flower. Or a tree seedling that pushes out of the dark soil into the sunshine. You find yourself inside. It's a feeling."

"Oh, I have a lot of feelings inside me."

"Of course you do! You're a—never mind. Let's get your feelings outside you so you can feel them in a bigger way."

"How?"

"With sound. Moving sound from inside to outside helps you take up space in the world and know how big you are."

"Oh, I can't do that. My mom always told me to be quiet. I can't be loud."

Emmy pondered as the fire snapped.

"What if we make sounds with you? Would that help?"

"Oh, I would like that very much."

"Okay. We want to make a sound that vibrates with our heart drum. The ah sound. Like the middle sound of the word star. St-*AH*-r."

Emmy looked around the circle. "Everyone, feel into your heart and follow me. We're going to breathe in, then make the *ah* sound all together. Soft at first. Then louder and louder."

Everyone nodded.

"Inhale and aahhhhhhhh, AAAAaaahhhhhHH, AAAHHHHHH!"

It worked. With each inhale and *ah* exhale, Speck grew bigger. His light burst into the air in blue and pink beams. Every breath was longer than the last. And louder. Soon, his voice was loudest. Emmy lifted her wing, signaling a pause.

"How do you feel?"

"Magnificent!"

"Lovely! And look how big you are!"

Speck was hovering over the circle, shining across the wide beach and river.

"Can we keep going, Emmy?"

"Of course! Let's ask for more help."

Emmy closed her eyes. She used her heart to connect with her planet—swimmy creatures, four-legged animals, winged ones, trees, wind, water, and land. She asked them all to pause and make the ah sound. One by one, they heard the call and agreed.

"Now, Speck, you start. Take the first breath."

He inhaled. "Ahhh, AaaaHHH, AAAaahhh, AAAHHHH!"

In a planetary cacophony of sound, each voice and vibration came together the way instruments and singers come together to form an orchestra.

Speck grew bigger, brighter, wider, and shinier. Bigger than Zander Mountain, bigger than the oceans, and higher than the clouds.

Emmy flew up next to him and lifted her wing, signaling a pause.

"Do you know what you are?" Emmy shouted.

"I'm a star!"

"Yes, you are. And only the sky can hold you. Ready to be full-size?"

"Yes!"

Emmy closed her eyes, sending the message to make the loudest sound possible. She inhaled the first breath.

"AAAAHHHHHHHHH-AHHH-AH-AHHH-AHH-AAAAAAAHHHHHHHHHH!"

Emmy's voice mixed with her dragon fire, propelling Speck past the atmosphere. Everyone on Hozho roared, chirped, and gurgled, making their loudest sounds.

Twinkle-Speck burst into full size as he rocketed into the night sky faster than he fell, leaving a streak of pink, blue, and white sparkles behind him. As he zoomed out of sight, Emmy heard him say, "Ali-star. My star name is Alistar! I'm ALISTAR!"

"I love you, Alistar," she said, blowing him a kiss as she turned back.

That night, Emmy rested. She curled her body around the stone circle with snoring gnomes and tinkling fairies sleeping on her. Yuki slept under her wing. She watched the glowing white and blue embers in the heart of the fire. She listened to Oyo's lullaby songs. She rolled her head and gazed at Alistar among the star-fires. She closed her sapphire-blue eyes and smiled.

Chapter 15

Amara and Her Mermaid
By Dr. Pamela J. Pine

"Hey, Stupid!"

"Hey, Ugly!"

"Hey, Amara-Go-Thara!"

Shy Amara approached the five kids who kept bothering her on her way to school. When they saw her, they immediately continued calling her names. As she got right close to them, rather than cross the street, she tried doing what her mom told her to do: keep her head up, have a peaceful face and body, and just walk on.

But the kids got bolder and started pushing her. One kid, the biggest of them all, pushed her so hard that she nearly fell. Luckily, Amara caught herself and walked on, but she was awfully close to crying.

When Amara got to school, she went straight to a hiding place that she'd discovered: the school gym locker room. Here, she could compose herself. No one ever came here before school at this time in the morning. Amara's hiding place was always a bit warm and humid and smelled like the ocean. It reminded Amara of where her family vacationed, which helped her relax.

*

Amara allowed herself a few tears. *Imagine yourself as strong and powerful,* she thought, commanding herself as she remembered her mom's words of encouragement. Amara's mom also suggested that she 'try on' being someone or something else that would help her feel strong.

Amara decided she would picture herself as a mermaid, swimming about in the warm, azure waters, among clams and sea stars—also known as starfish, but since the ones in her mind shone silver and gold, 'sea stars' was a much better term, she thought—and beautiful yellow and black striped fish and other ones that looked like swimming rainbows!

As she sat there, imagining, she heard someone speak.

"Come closer, Amara," called a woman's voice, all silky smooth and kind.

"I can help you," said the voice.

There was an old-fashioned bathtub in the girls' locker room that was a holdover from a much earlier time in this old school. You know the kind of tub, or maybe you've seen pictures of one, an oval-shaped tub with four legs and a very deep bathing space?

"What are you waiting for?" called the cheery voice from the tub.

Understandably, this was a bit unsettling for Amara, and she thought, perhaps, given all the stress she was under, that she was hallucinating and hearing things that were not there.

Amara delicately crossed the black, rubber-tile-covered floor to see whether there was, indeed, someone there. She got a little closer and noticed two beautiful, gleaming, multi-colored fins bent and sticking up on one end of the tub. Amara gave a little gasp, which brought a little giggle from whatever was in that tub, while some rainbow-glistening bubbles rose in the air.

Amara got a little closer and then close enough to peer inside the bath to see beyond its rim.

Inside, a beautiful, shining, smiling mermaid was relaxing and enjoying the warm bubble bath water.

The mermaid was beautiful and had all those qualities that common mermaids have. She was long, from the top of her magical head to the bottom of her tail fins. She had lean but powerful arms to propel her through the water, a ballerina's body that Amara imagined could easily move around rocks and seaweed near the ocean floor, and a large, flexible, shimmering, scaled tail that stretched from her waist down to her two tail fins—with which, Amara thought, she'd be able, at a mere flick, to change directions in a flash. And she had flowing, elegant hair.

"Uh, hello?" said Amara.

"Well, hello," said Elin the mermaid with a warm smile.

"Who, please, are you?" said Amara, who was, after all, a polite girl.

"I am Elin, your *I-Am-Your-Being Mermaid*. I live through you, and I am here to help."

Amara had read stories about mermaids and loved the way they looked as well as their magical powers, but never imagined she'd ever meet one!

Elin propped herself up with her upper arms on the rim of the tub and said, "Amara, I am *your* being mermaid. We are rare. There is one quality that we have that no other mermaid has. You can call on us inside your mind, and we will be there, just like that, to help you if you need help. We come to you the way you need us to, to help rescue our friends from difficult feelings and situations and help them understand how to deal with them."

"You called me, so I came," she smiled. "I can help you. I know you've been having some difficulties with the five kids at school, so I've come to take you on a little journey and help you see what's beyond. I think that might be useful in dealing with those kids and other difficult experiences in the future."

Amara looked at her watch nervously. "Don't worry," said Elin with a small smile, "I will have you back in time for the start of school."

Amara had been taught to be somewhat cautious, but something told her that this trip with Elin would be okay.

"Come on in, Amara. The water is lovely. Close your eyes. Think of the ocean. It's a beautiful color blue, it's warm, there are exquisitely colored fish, sea stars, and the sun is shining," It was just as Amara was imagining it!

Well, thought Amara, *this is very odd,* but swung a leg over the side of the tub. As soon as her foot touched the water, Amara and Elin were both transported.

*

Amara found herself in the ocean, swimming around. She could stay under the water with no problem at all and had turned into quite the strong swimmer.

Elin told her, "You have no enemies here. You only have your strength and the beauty that surrounds you. You can go wherever you want, and no one will harm you. But I do want to show you around a bit."

144 |

Elin told Amara to follow her down some depths. Amara followed, gliding easily.

Beauty reigned all around them, from the color of the water to the many shades of orange, red, and pink coral. Even the tint of green seaweed that stemmed from the ocean shelves seemed unusually bright, and doubly so when the sun shown on it through the water.

It was getting darker the further they swam, but there was still enough light for Amara to see. When Elin and Amara landed upon the ocean floor, they arrived at a place that had been covered with various types of shells and stones.

"Amara," said Elin, "I want to introduce you to a friend of mine, Ethan'O." And with that, Elin called out, "Oh, Ethan'O, please come meet a friend."

The giant Pacific octopus startled Amara when he emerged from his den, moving aside the various shells and stones that helped protect him and his den. He was enormous and reddish pink, which made him seem even more imposing, particularly given all those arms!

Ethan'O emerged with what Amara could only describe as a smile and a sense of warmth. Amara had learned about octopuses and knew they were strong but rarely harmful to people. They were smart, resourceful, and even playful and were able to make friends with people. She also knew that, incredibly, they had three hearts, and she imagined that Ethan'O's must be gigantic.

Once all of Ethan'O was fully out (it took a while given his size), he gave Amara a nod, moved his head back, and presented a bubbly, "It's nice to make your acquaintance, Amara."

Elin proceeded to explain the problems that Amara was having and hoped Ethan'O could help Amara.

Ethan'O looked at Amara and, with the tip of one arm, patted a bend in another, inviting Amara to sit. With just the slightest hesitation, Amara took a seat on the soft 'knee' of the octopus, looking sad to have heard her story relayed back to her.

Ethan'O and Elin asked questions about what had happened in the past, what it felt like, whether she thought she knew any solutions, and what she might do upon her return to school, which Amara thought must nearly be over by now! Sometimes Amara cried because it all felt so wrong and unfair and hurt her feelings so!

Both Elin and Ethan'O pointed out a few very important things for Amara to think about. They said that both little beings and adults hold within them the ability to be kind and cruel.

"It's largely a part of human nature," said Elin.

"But why?" asked Amara.

"That," said Ethan'O, "is a much longer story," and smiled a wide, sweet smile.

"It's important to understand," Ethan'O continued, "that we need to trust our intuition."

"What do you mean?" asked Amara.

Elin explained, "Intuition is how we react to situations *in our gut*—it's how something makes our brain, heart, stomach, and whole body feel. While we want to be kind and understanding, we also must protect ourselves."

Erin continued, "When people are small and have tried to do what they can think of, like walking away or taking a different path, it's time to get other, more powerful people involved. We'd like to suggest that you speak with your teachers, tell them what has been going on, and ask them to speak to their classes, teach the students about bullying, think of why it happens, how it feels, why it is so wrong, and tell all the students about consequences—what will happen to students if they mistreat other students. Maybe you can even suggest ways to do this, like play-acting. You can ask them not to use your name if you want. If it does not stop, Amara, you must go to a person in charge, and that may be the principal."

Amara considered this, and after a pause, Elin said, "It's time to go back now, Amara."

"Remember," said Ethan'O, "your true strength comes from within."

Amara had made two real friends. She gave a squishy goodbye hug to Ethan'O and thanked him for listening and helping her work through what to do.

Elin and Amara swam toward the surface as the light got brighter and brighter. As they broke the surface, Amara found herself back in the locker room ten minutes before the day's classes began!

*

Amara decided to go into the classroom early and asked her teacher if she might have a few minutes before class time to talk with her about something important to her safety.

The teacher looked a bit startled and worried at the same time but said, "Of course."

"I'm being bullied regularly in school and on my way to and from school, and I need your help, please. Can we meet later today, maybe with other teachers, to figure out what to do?"

"Of course," the teacher said again. "I'm sorry this is happening to you, Amara."

By the end of school, her teacher had spoken to other teachers and decided to plan a program to speak to all the students in the school. She called Amara's mom for a ride home that day and waited with her after school until her mom came.

Amara stayed in touch with Elin who was always there to help Amara navigate her world any time she needed a hand. Amara was always grateful for her help and she grew into a strong and confident woman who came to not only understand the ways of the world but to navigate the hard parts of it when they came along.

Chapter 16

Mia The Curious Cat Makes Her Mark

By TJ STAR

My name is Mia, and I'm a spotted cat from Tkaronto, Canada, though my family is from an ancient lineage in South Asia.

I'm excited. It's the first day of school in the Tkaronto Jungle, and this new school year, I'm getting a new teacher. As a cat, I have so much energy and always have the urge to explore. We cats like moving around;

we're active and always curious to see what's around us. This is why I cannot stay put!

My family moved to the Tkaronto Jungle many generations ago. Tkaronto is a magical place full of so many different types of animals. I love going with my animal friends to the center where there is so much happening. Tkaronto is so colorful with animals from all over the world and is part of the bigger ecosystem of Canada. The name Tkaronto comes from the Mohawk culture and means the place in the water where the trees are standing.

I have not met other spotted cats like me in Tkaronto, but there are so many other cool animals in the jungle, from hummingbirds to gorillas to chimpanzees, parrots, and even jaguars. My best friends in the jungle are Tina the toucan and Oscar the orangutan, whom I met at jungle school.

Tina is bright, yellow, full of life, and she is always talking.

Oscar is orange, quiet, and one of the warmest animals I know.

Tina and Oscar never get bored of me, as I always take them on adventures.

As we wait in line outside our jungle class, I see a sign go up that says Ms. Kay will be our new teacher for the year. She has been around the whole world and lived in many other jungles.

We hear the chirping call to go inside. As we enter, Ms. Kay appears at the front of the class. She is just as bold and colorful as I imagined. What makes me excited to see is that she is also a cat but orange in color and has black stripes!

"Welcome to a new school year, jungle students! Before we begin and talk about what we're learning this year, I want to get to know who you are as animals. I want you all to think about what inspires you and share this with the class. Ask yourself, how would I like to make my mark in the world? Take some time to write it down," Ms. Kay said.

Tina raised her wing, "Ms. Kay, do you mean, what do we want to be in the world, because I already know! I want to have my own singing show!" sang Tina.

"I can hear that, Tina! Class, I want you to tell me how you would like to make an impact in the world. What makes you who you are?" Ms. Kay asked with a smile.

Ms. Kay then locked eyes with me. I started getting nervous because I didn't know what to say.

"What about you, Mia?" asked Ms. Kay

"Well, I'm not sure yet, Mrs. Kay, but I like exploring and want to see the world one day just like you!" I said.

"Wow, Mia, that is amazing! See, class, you don't have to know exactly what you want to do, but there is something deep inside that makes us happy. Your mark is what you would like to impact the world. I hope you keep exploring Mia and see the world one day. The explorer in me sees the explorer in you!" said Ms. Kay.

I have never had anyone call me an explorer before!

That's it! I am making my mark as an explorer! I couldn't stop smiling.

I thought to myself about what my parents shared about Tkaranto. Mom and Dad always told me that because Tkaranto is so big, it's good to stay close to home.

"Many things can happen in the jungle, both good and bad, Mia," Dad would always say, "It's the best teacher, after all."

"It's better to be closer to the den, your safe at home," Mom would say.

"So, it's better to go as a *family* and explore the jungle and learn more about this beautiful place we call home," Dad would add.

As I drift back to the classroom, Ms. Kay heads to the front.

"Okay, class," said Ms. Kay as she sat down, "I will give you a few minutes to continue writing down what inspires you."

I can't believe Ms. Kay and I are both cats, and it's so interesting that we both have different patterns.,I thought as I began to write down how I would like to make my mark in the world. *I know I want to explore the world and also show others how to explore it too! That will be my impact. But I want to start with exploring myself.*

I decided to go by Ms. Kay's desk and asked, "Ms. Kay, how come we are both cats, but you have stripes and I have spots?"

"Well, Mia, many of us who live in Tkaronto have heritage in another part of the bigger world. Do you know what heritage means, Mia?"

"I think so. Does it mean where our families come from?" I asked.

"Yes, Mia. You see, my family originally are from Egypt, and we are from an ancient lineage of Mau cats. How about you, Mia? Do you know where your family originated from?"

"I've never heard of this place before! That is so cool! I wonder if it's the same with my family. My family has spots, but not a lot of cats here have the same spots as us; we are different from them," I said.

"You should ask your parents, Mia, it's important to know our roots, where we came from. It was so nice to learn that you like exploring," said Ms. Kay. "Enjoy the rest of your day."

"Thanks, Ms. Kay! I'm looking forward to finding out about my roots and learning from you for the rest of the year!" I said as I waved goodbye and headed home.

When I got in, Dad greeted me, but he was not very happy. "Mia! Where have you been?! You were not with your friends after school, and you didn't come home!"

"I'm sorry, Dad, I wanted to stay behind and chat with Ms. Kay, our new teacher, and I didn't realize the time and that it was getting dark outside."

"Mia, what do I always tell you? It's not safe to come home late. The jungle is dangerous at night, Mia."

"I'm sorry Dad," I said as I hugged him. "Guess what?! I met Ms. Kay today, and she told me to ask where we are from. She is a cat too, but she doesn't look like us! She is orange and has black stripes. We are brown and have spots."

"Mia, there are only a few of us jungle cats, and we must remember our heritage here in Tkaronto," Dad said proudly.

"Dad, I'd like to know why we are here and which part of the world is our ancient lineage from?" I said.

"Well Mia, we are from a different part of the world where it became unsafe for us, so we decided to come to Tkaronto for a better life. Our family is from an ancient lineage of jungle cats. Our lineage goes as far back as when Africa and South Asia were connected. Legend has it that we are originally from a sunken land called Lumeria. Spotted jungle cats like us used to rule the land. In recent times, our family migrated to northern Sri Lanka and Southern India. There is not much of our breed left as we have mixed with many other cat breeds," Dad said.

"Is that why our spots are different?" I asked.

"Yes, Mia. I'm very proud our family has passed down our roots for thousands of years and maintained our unique spots. Not many jungle cats these days have our spots. Mia, promise me you'll remember where we come from. Never forget that!" said Dad.

"I will, Dad. I want to go and see where we are from one day. Dad, there must be so many other ancient jungles out there, but I want to see ours first and explore our heritage!" I exclaimed.

"Mia, our jungle is no more, but we can see where our ancestors migrated. I have faith that you will see this one day!" said Dad.

"Thanks, Dad, I'm happy you shared this with me," I said and purred with affection.

How cool is it that my ancestors are from a sunken jungle kingdom? I knew I was different. These spots are special.

I start making my way to bed and close my eyes.

Tonight, I will make a wish.

Star light, star bright, the first star I see tonight. I wish I may, I wish I might, have this wish I wish tonight. . .

. . . I wish to be an explorer, to discover all the jungles in the world one day, share this curiosity with others, and take them on many, many journeys with me.

As I keep wishing, I start to see Ms. Kay with me on the road, holding my paw as she gives me a map. Tina and Oscar appear, and we are on our way down the road, ready to explore!

"That's the spirit, Mia! I know you will be brilliant out there! I know it," Ms. Kay said as she purred and hugged me. I waved goodbye with a big smile and continued on the road into the horizon on my own.

"MIA! TIME TO GET READY FOR BED!" Dad loudly meowed.

I slowly get out of my bed, grab my journal, and start writing with a big smile on my face.

I am going to make my mark as an explorer and discover all the jungles and ecosystems in the world!

We all have something that sparks and makes us come alive.

For me, it is exploring and being curious.

Find your spark and let it be your personal power. Continue exploring and being curious as it connects us to everything around us.

Love Mia, the wild Rusty-spotted cat.

Chapter 17

Magical Times with Grandpa in His Enchanting Garden
Discovering Valuable Treasures for Life
By Dr. Charleen M. Michel

Enchanting flowers,
Fragrant Garden Memories,
Dancing in the sun.

" I need your help in the house."

"Sorry, Grandma, I can't," I put my hands on my hips. "I've more important things to do with Grandpa."

Hi, my name's Michelle. I've been passionate about gardening since I was a little girl. Now I'm more than 60 years old and have played in gardens my whole life. Here's my story about being in an enchanting garden with my grandpa.

*

There was something magical about being in the fresh air with the birds, butterflies, and flowers. In the garden, beautiful fragrances tickled my nose, and colors captured my eye, especially when the warm, bright sun was shining. I loved feeling the dirt on my hands. It was like finger painting.

In the garden, I was happy and free. I was at home, and it felt so good!

From the time I was six until I was a teenager, I spent my summer vacation at my grandparents' home. Grandma wanted my help in the house, and Grandpa wanted my help in his garden.

My choice was simple as I declared: "I, Michelle, want to be in the garden with my grandpa."

Grandpa was a big man at six feet two inches, or 1.87 meters tall.

I was just a small girl at nearly three feet or one meter tall.

When we were alone, he called me his little Rosebud. It was our secret, and I felt special. During the day, he worked in the nursery across the street. When he came home, his hands were rough, and his clothes were dirty.

All that matters is he wants to spend time with me in his garden, I thought.

One day, Grandpa came home from work and brought me a small crème colored watering can painted with a pink rose. It was a prized treasure and just perfect for me.

"Grandpa, Let's go! I'm ready to water the plants," I said with twinkling eyes. I put on my garden apron, printed with bright red roses, and proudly hugged my new watering can.

"Michelle, today you can kick off your socks and shoes and walk barefoot in the grass," Grandpa explained.

"Whoopee!" I giggled as I danced in the garden with the grass tickling my feet.

"This is so COOOOOOL!" I replied.

Suddenly I screamed, "Oh no! A huge frog. Go away, Mr. Frog."

"He won't hurt you. He wants to play, too," Grandpa said as he moved it away.

"Whew! That's much better," I said. "Thank you, Grandpa."

We smiled, and he hugged me.

We spent each sunny afternoon together in the garden, and I developed a nice suntan and rosy cheeks. I felt beautiful whenever I was with him.

Grandpa's garden was a paradise, with a white fence at the entrance and a narrow path that connected the flower beds. Some beds were filled with petunias, and others with roses. Between the paths was lush, green grass. At the back of the garden was a garden shed. If you looked beyond the shed, you'd discover a white swing glistening in the sun, waiting to welcome its guests. Long, straight green hedges outlined the garden's boundaries.

"Today, we'll start with the white and purple petunias. They're my favorites. Put your finger in the soil, Michelle, to see if it's moist," He explained.

"Ugh, what if there's a worm in the dirt? They're slimy. Worms are for fishing, not gardening, Grandpa," I responded.

"Don't worry. They won't eat you. They like other food." He smiled.

Bravely, I put one finger in the dirt.

Whew. No worms here. Only a dirty finger.

"Grandpa, the dirt's not moist; it's dry and needs water," I said.

He replied, "Why don't you water it?"

I filled my watering can and gently watered each petunia. "The watering's all done!" I confirmed.

"Michelle, do you see how some flowers are faded?" he asked. "We pinch them away with our thumb and index finger. I'll show you. Do you want to try?"

"Yes, I do. It looks simple enough," I replied.

"Oh no! What have I done?" I screamed as I discovered a huge hole between the plants.

I started to cry. "I can't do this! I killed them."

Grandpa wiped the tears from my cheeks and gave me a big hug. "Don't worry, they'll grow back," he assured me.

Each day afterward, I checked on the petunias. After a week, they grew back, and I danced with joy. Everyone said Grandpa had the most beautiful petunias in the whole wide world. I knew he did. I helped him!

The next flower bed on today's garden route was a beautiful centerpiece in the middle of the garden. Even the bees and butterflies liked to dance and play here. Grandpa explained, "This is my new rose bed. The roses are called Fragrant Cloud."

The large, coral-red roses caught my eye. "I must get a closer look," I said with excitement. My nose tingled, and I was immediately enchanted by their graceful presence and delightful fragrance. They smelled citrus fruity, pumpkin spicy, and everything nicey.

"Grandpa, they give me goosebumps. I want them in my garden when I grow up."

Grandpa smiled. "The rose fragrance is used for perfume," he explained.

I immediately knew I wanted rose-fragrant perfume for the rest of my life, and when I got older, I always did.

"Look, the busy-buzzy-bees also like them," he said.

"Oh no. Bees. I don't want to be stung."

"If you don't bother them, Michelle, they won't bother you," Grandpa assured me. He explained, "Caring for roses requires special attention. They need a lot of water, but not *on* the rose petals, only at the *base* of the plant. We must remove the fallen leaves and petals from the ground."

I confirmed, "Got it, I'll take them away."

"Then we put special rose food around the base and work it into the soil."

"I can do that. I'll give them food and water," I replied. When the feeding was done, Grandpa explained, "To cut the roses, we use special garden scissors. We cut them just above the thorn, and two leaves under the wilting rose."

There were lots of beautiful roses, little rosebuds, wilting roses, and lots of thorns.

"OUCH!" A thorn stuck in my finger, and it started to bleed. "Grandpa, I'll let you cut these."

Grandpa lovingly removed the thorn from my finger, and the bleeding stopped. He kissed my forehead and gave me a big hug. "Rosebud, you should practice for your garden later. With all the day's excitement, I forgot to give you the small leather gloves with red roses to protect your hands. They're waiting for you on the table in the garden shed. They match your apron. I also bought smaller garden scissors for your little hands. Why don't you go and get them."

I ran to the shed, put on the gloves, and picked up the scissors.

"Grandpa, they're just perfect for me," I said proudly as I returned.

I took a deep breath and made my first cut above the finger-piercing thorns.

"Hmm, not bad," he said. "You've got talent. Let's cut the rest. Practice makes perfect!"

Soon afterward, the roses were nurtured, and they smelled delicious.

"Roses are my favorite, Grandpa!" My eyes danced with joy.

"Let's cut some roses to enjoy later." He smiled as we cut a few roses, and I danced into the house to put them into a vase.

Grandma tried to hold me back, "Where are you going, young lady? Where are your shoes? Your feet are dirty, and your apron is filthy. You must take a bath, and I must wash your clothes!"

"I'm out of here. I still have important things to do. Grandpa needs me." I pretended not to hear her and raced outside before she could grab me.

"Back so soon?" Grandpa said with surprise. "I need help repairing the wooden fence. Let's find a hammer and some nails."

"Grandpa, I don't know how to use a hammer," I said.

"I'll show you. Here's a small one just for you," he responded.

bang, Bang, B A N G !

I declared, "All done!"

Grandpa clarified, "Almost, we still need to paint the fence. Let's get some white paint and a paintbrush."

"I'm tired. Can we go for ice cream?" I asked.

"We just need a few more minutes. Here's a smaller paintbrush for you."

"I learned to paint in my art classes, so I've got this," I said.

Ten minutes later, the garden smelled of fresh paint, and we finished our gardening for the day. We cleaned the tools and put them in the garden shed. Afterward, we washed our hands, and I washed my feet. I removed my filthy apron and dropped it on the back porch.

Grandma can wash it later.

Oops, I almost forgot, I must put on my socks and shoes.

Grandpa announced, "Now it's time for our ice cream to celebrate."

"Yippie! I love ice cream. It's my favorite food," I declared.

Grandpa smiled and replied, "Mine too!"

We rushed into the house, grabbed two vanilla ice cream cones from the freezer, and quickly snuck back to the garden. We sat alone on the garden swing, admiring our work. There was no one to bother us.

I licked my ice cream and shouted with joy, "YUMMY!"

Grandpa nodded.

I closed my eyes and took a few deep breaths. The smell of fragrant roses and the freshly painted fence filled the air.

The birds sang, the bees buzzed, and the butterflies fluttered from flower to flower as they danced—an enchanting garden ballet.

Wow, what a great day. I love being with my grandpa in his garden.

Someday I'll have my own garden with lots of roses.

I can hardly wait.

That night, after my bath, before falling asleep, my heart overflowed with delight. I thought about all the smiles we exchanged during the day. Even when I made a mistake, was scared, or hurt, I still felt loved and cherished from the big hugs we shared. I remembered Grandpa's patience as he took the time to show me what to do.

As my eyes softly closed, I recalled the magical moments, the fragrant memories, and dancing in the sun.

I smiled and drifted off to sleep, as I thought. . .

HE'S SIMPLY THE BEST!

Chapter 18

The Wisdom of Nature
Messages for Mia
By MJ Luna

Dingggggg, chimed the dismissal bell.

Mia was looking forward to leaving school. It had been a month since the start of the school year without her best friend, Jasper.

Jasper's family moved out of state last summer. The day they said goodbye seemed like the worst day of her life.

She felt a heaviness on her chest that day, and it hadn't changed much. The emotions of sadness and feeling alone washed over her every day.

Last year during recess, when her classmates were climbing on the play equipment or playing games on the blacktop, Mia and Jasper were in the field intently watching ants construct their homes, catching toads and grasshoppers, and building houses for chipmunks made of leaves and twigs.

Since Jasper left, it hadn't felt the same, and Mia often sat by herself in the field at school.

SLAM! Mia carelessly let the screen door go behind her as she entered the back door to her home. She sluggishly pulled out a chair from the kitchen table to settle into.

"Mia!" bellowed her mother. "Wash your hands and have your snack quickly. We're going to visit Grandmother, and you're having an overnight stay with her."

"YAY!" Mia's spirits were suddenly lifted.

Grandmother always listened to Mia when they visited and wanted to know what new discoveries she'd made in nature.

After Mia and her parents had arrived at Grandmother's house and hugs were exchanged, Grandmother asked, "Mia, what new and fascinating life forms have you discovered since I saw you last?"

Mia paused for a moment, then proudly replied, "I watched a brown spider spin its web in the garden yesterday! It didn't take her that long, and it was *sooooo* big when it was done!"

"That's wonderful! I'm glad you took the time to watch!" She then asked, "What have you been spinning in *your* web?"

Mia knew what Grandmother meant. "Well, I've been feeling a little down since Jasper moved. I really miss him," Mia said in a somber voice. "School hasn't been the same. There doesn't seem to be any other kids interested in what I like to do."

Grandmother replied, "It's natural to feel that way when someone close to you has moved, and you don't see them every day like you used to. It's okay to feel sadness, Mia."

"Mom says we can visit him and his family during winter break."

"That's something to look forward to and be grateful for!"

"Yes, it is," replied Mia, feeling a little better about the situation.

Grandmother switched the focus to tomorrow's events.

"We're having breakfast early tomorrow, so we can go on a long hike into the forest. Make sure you get some good sleep tonight."

"Yippee!"

Mia loved going on adventures with Grandmother, especially in the forest!

After breakfast the next morning, Mia and Grandmother walked towards the field. Mia was excited to be in nature as her senses always seemed sharper and more attuned. She remembered a conversation she had with Grandmother the last time they hiked. She explained that the bees, butterflies, and flowers all work together so more plants can grow the next season and serve as food for many creatures. Grandmother always shared an interesting piece of knowledge with Mia when they were together.

I wonder what she'll be sharing today?

Just as she finished this thought, Grandmother said, "I have a surprise for you!"

Mia bubbled with eagerness to hear what Grandmother was going to reveal.

"We're going deeper into the forest to some places you've never seen before."

"WOW! What will we see?" Mia enthusiastically asked.

"Animals' homes and maybe we'll catch a glimpse of the animals themselves."

"What animals?"

"You'll see," said Grandmother.

Mia could hardly contain her exhilaration as she started skipping up the path. As they reached the edge of the forest, two gray squirrels dashed in front of them.

"Look at them chasing each other!" declared Mia. "They look like they're playing tag!"

She watched them as they scurried up an oak tree—around and around the tree they went!

"That's very observant of you, Mia. I'm glad you're noticing these important things."

Grandmother explained that noticing the traits and behaviors of animals or any other living form come as signs and messages to us. And because we're all living creatures, we have the same qualities.

"The squirrels tell us that it's important to be playful, even as we get older, because it brings joy and happiness into our lives. Animals make their presence known to us whether we see, hear, or even smell them, and it's usually just when we need their message. They are reminders of our strengths and abilities."

Grandmother asked Mia, "How does it make you feel when you see the squirrels playing?"

"It makes me happy and makes *me* want to play."

"Wonderful! So, what will you do during recess when you get back to school?"

"I will play!" Mia said gleefully.

They came to a stream and hopped across the stones to get to the other side and walked much further than Mia had been in the past with Grandmother. They eventually came to an opening to see a vast meadow.

"Shhhh," Grandmother placed her finger close to her lips and whispered, "as we walk along the edge, keep looking out into the field."

Mia's eyes were wide open with anticipation of what she might see. They walked almost to the end; then Mia spotted something in the distance.

"I see one, two, three, four, *five* deer!" Mia exclaimed, trying to stay quiet.

The deer looked in their direction with their perked ears. Mia and Grandmother stayed still as the deer returned to grazing after a few moments. Mia saw that three of the deer were young fawns, as they still had white spots on their fur. The other two seemed to be the mothers as they were much bigger. They stayed close to the fawns, tending to them with nudges and licks.

Mia and Grandmother eventually moved on to the shade of the forest. Grandmother asked, "What message do you think the deer brought to you?"

Mia recalled what Grandmother told her to look for when animals show up. "They have great hearing. And the mothers seemed very caring towards the babies."

"Great observations, Mia! Deer send a message of sensitivity, kindness, and gentleness," affirmed Grandmother.

She went on to say, "The emotions of sadness and loneliness you've been feeling since Jasper moved away are another type of sensitivity and are actually a gift that you should be proud of.

Emotions allow us to feel and work through our challenges in a healthy way. So be kind and gentle with yourself while you're feeling this way; your body will know when it is time to shift and feel better."

Mia was already feeling better and knew deep down that Jasper would always be her friend. *He just lives further away and goes to a different school now,* she thought.

They continued walking and eventually came upon a pond surrounded by evergreen trees. At one end, Mia noticed a huge mound of sticks.

"What's that?" Mia asked Grandmother. "That is a lodge, the home of a beaver."

Suddenly, Mia spotted something in the water heading towards the lodge. "Look! It's a beaver climbing up on the lodge, and it looks like it has sticks in its mouth!"

"That's great! I was hoping the beaver would show up for us today."

Grandmother continued, "Beavers are hard workers, and they dedicate a lot of time to building their homes. They show us that anything is possible if we put steady effort towards it."

As Grandmother finished her sentence, Mia noticed a large bird flying in the sky; it swooped into the pond and then took flight again. It looked as though it was holding a fish in its talons.

"WOW! Did you see that, Grandmother!" Mia bellowed as she couldn't contain her excitement. "It looks like a bald eagle!"

Grandmother looked to the sky, "Yes, you are right!"

"Look how big it is!"

Mia was in awe of the size of the eagle with its long wingspan. They watched it circle around and land in a large stick nest atop a barren tree.

"You can see it eating the fish!"

"What are you learning from the eagle?" asked Grandmother.

"It seemed like it knew it wanted that fish and caught it."

"Yes, eagles send a message of determination. If you want something, you have to go after it. How did it make you feel when you saw it flying?"

Mia had difficulty finding the words but finally said, "It almost took my breath away!"

"Yes, it was impressive," said Grandmother. "The eagle sends a message of spreading your wings, showing your true self to the world, and being proud of who you are. We all have gifts and talents to share with others."

"Well, we've had quite a treat today with all the animals that have shown up for us," proclaimed Grandmother. "We'll stop at the stream on our way back so you can make a wish."

Mia learned from Grandmother a while ago that creating a picture in your mind, saying what you want, feeling how it feels, and sending it with the flowing water makes the wish come true.

Mia was quiet on the hike back to the stream as she thought of all the things she had learned from Grandmother today.

As they approached the stream, Mia was ready to state her wish. She closed her eyes and pictured herself playing with new friends in the field at school, watching insects, catching creatures, building animal homes, and felt the joy it brought her.

"I wish for new friends to play with in the field at school," Mia declared.

"That's a great wish! How will you help that wish come true?"

"I'll ask other kids to play in the field and show them how to make chipmunk houses."

"Wonderful," said Grandmother.

"What if there's a day they want to play tag instead?"

Mia thought for a moment and then said, "I will be kind and play what others like, too."

Mia returned to school feeling so much better. She asked other kids to play in the field, and some came. She taught them how to make chipmunk houses. There were other days when she played tag and games on the blacktop, too.

One day, Mia's teacher introduced a new student to their class.

"This is Troy," announced Mia's teacher. "He just moved here from out of state, and he tells me he loves nature!"

Mia's ears perked up, and she knew exactly who she was going to ask to play with her in the field today.

Wish granted!

Hope you enjoyed the story! I enjoyed it writing it thoroughly!

MJ Luna

Chapter 19

Twig and Terri
Learn to Love Through Loss
By Terri Hawke

W hat am I doing? I've held, hugged, talked to, comforted, and loved on every age, color, and size of cat in this shelter! And it's almost time for them to close. Wait.

Who's that?

Who's the little black and white kitten at the front of the cage eating and kneading the blanket under the bowl of kibble?

How adorable! I hadn't seen that kitten before.

I open the cage door and pick him up. The black and white kitten snuggles into my arms, purring so loudly he drowns out the meowing of the other cats and kittens. He's so soft and beautiful. In that moment, I knew this was the one.

Whoa! She noticed me. She's coming over to my cage!

She's holding me. Oh, she's so cuddly.

I'm so glad I stopped sleeping and decided to get a nibble of kibble.

After meeting him, I headed to the animal shelter's front desk, and I told them Copper was the kitten I wanted to adopt! That was the name written on his cage. When I brought the six-month-old Copper home, I decided to change his name. I wanted his new name to fit him and fit in with our cat clowder. The clowder of kitties was Sage, Pinecone, Marbles, and Lovebug. Copper, the only male cat, became Twig.

I have the best name of all!

*This place is a cat paradise. So
many toys to chase and bite
and bat, and cat scratchies to
sharpen my claws on, and cat
trees to climb high upon.*

*My person, who is called Terri,
is such a great cat person.*

I'm gonna love it here!

We bonded quickly and deeply and became best friends. I found
this long-haired white cat with black splotches to be my soul
kitty, my heart kitty. Twig was an indoor cat which kept him safe
his entire life. He was a goofball, making every empty box his
favorite toy to hide and curl up in. Every bag was a giant mouse
needing to be attacked. And he loved spa day, lying on a towel
in the bathroom while I took a shower. *How did I get so lucky to
find such a playful, cuddly, soft cat?*

*I'm a little jealous of those other
kitties in this clowder. But I
know I'm her favorite. We'll be
together a long time, and I'll
take care of her, just like she
takes care of me.*

Twig and I had to move away from those kitties. We moved
three times. Every time we moved, he settled right in and
climbed to the top of his cat tree to survey his new digs.

When I adopted Templeton, the Pomeranian-chihuahua, Twig took right to him, and they became best buddies.

Who is this guy?

He's a little smaller than me and fluffier but warm and soft and silly.

This new dog she adopted is pretty cool.

I think I'm going to like him. He'll make a warm cuddler.

Many years after adopting Twig, I lost my parents at different times. It was tough for me. I cried and was stunned when I realized they were gone. Like other people and animals I had lost, I was sad, angry, and even a little scared. But Twig was there, taking up his favorite place on the left side of my chest, purring away. Our heartbeats became one, my breath slowing as he comforted me.

My favorite place to be is lying on the left side of her chest, purring loudly and cuddling closely with her.

I feel our heartbeats become one. I feel her breathing slow down as she calms down.

After my mom died, when I was much older, I left Twig at home for a few days with a sitter. I went where I always go when I'm sad, out in nature. This time, it was to the ocean. I took Templeton with me for company since Twig wasn't a fan of travel. It rained most of the time, but it was good to get away and heal. The fresh air and scent of saltwater calmed my mind. I became the brown pelicans I saw cruising effortlessly over the tops of the crashing waves. I felt as if the waves were washing away the pain of losing my mom.

Where did Terri and Templeton go?

I remember, Terri said they were going to the ocean to heal, and I should stay home because it's a long journey for a cat like me who does not like the car and traveling.

I miss them. I'll be happier when they both return.

She always comes back and gives me big, gentle hugs.

I'll give her lots of love and purrs when she gets home.

When my dad died, I pushed my face into Twig's fur and cried. I missed my parents. Losing companion animals and humans I love makes me sad. My companion animals give me comfort.

Walking in nature gives me healing. Writing in a journal helps me process sorrow. Finding photographs and hanging a few up also helps me. Sometimes, the photos make me cry; sometimes, they make me smile.

I wonder why water is coming out of her eyes.

Now she is burying her face in my soft fur and is making a funny noise with more water coming out of her eyes.

I'm glad I could be here for her. I'm going to curl up next to her and share my love.

She's petting me, running her hand gently and slowly over my fur. We connect.

I went for a long walk in the forest to think about losing Dad and to just be in the forest, in nature. I smelled the fresh scent of the Douglas-fir tree needles. I found a banana slug munching on detritus (dead plant stuff) breaking it down into soil. I could hear so many birds singing as they sang out to attract a mate and to start building nests. I stopped to hug a big Grandmother fir. I could feel the healing energy of her and the entire forest as I walked slowly, stopping to lean into the moments.

One day an orange and black butterfly was fluttering around the backyard and kept landing on my head. It's one of my favorite butterflies—the Red Admiral! The larva is found on nettles, where it lays its eggs. The butterfly feeds on the nectar of many types of flowers, including asters. Sadly, I had neither of these at this house. But why did it keep landing on my head?

Was it Mom letting me know she was still watching over me? Or is Dad stopping by to say hi? I don't know who it was, but seeing it and having it land on me made me smile.

I can see her playing with a fluttery thing. Oh, how I wish I could go out in the backyard and chase it and catch it! I'll just have to be content sitting here staring out the sliding glass door and enjoying the twinkle in her eye.

A couple of years later, Twig wasn't feeling well, and I had to rush him to the emergency veterinarian. They found out his big, beautiful heart wasn't working right. We put him on medication to help make him feel better. It worked for a while, but not long enough.

I feel weird. My insides don't feel right.

I'm confused. What is happening to me?

Terri's trying to put these pills in my food and down my throat, but it's not working very well.

I don't think I'm gonna be here a lot longer; it's just a feeling I am having.

I'm so tired.

Twig did well for a few months, but his heart gave out. Twig died, and a little bit of me felt like it did, too. I decided not to ignore my feelings and to feel the sadness and the anger over losing him, so I cried my eyes out. After all of that crying, I still cried more. I was still sad and sometimes mad because I lost my best friend. I was forgetful and sometimes couldn't concentrate because of this. Twig was my heart kitty. He was always there for me. And now he was gone.

I had Twig cremated and the ashes put in a little box. They clipped some of his fur off and took an imprint of his paw for me. I put those in a special frame with a beautiful photograph of Twig and hung it on my wall. I feel close to him when I see the memorial I created for him and smile.

I see. I feel. But I'm not there.

My little kitty soul has moved on and crossed the rainbow bridge.

I miss Terri but it was time for me to leave.

I'll let her know I'm watching over her by showing up sometimes when she needs me the most.

Someday, Terri, we will meet again.

I went to the forest again to inhale the pungent scent of skunk cabbage. I watched a yellow-spotted millipede plod along, then suddenly curl up to protect itself, although that's not a problem since it's covered in a tiny bit of cyanide. I spot several warblers flitting from branch to branch, catching tiny insects unseen to our eyes. I heard the calming sound of a babbling stream creating damp areas for Pacific giant salamanders. My heart sings when I'm in the forest, and it helps me heal.

Sometimes, I see Twig out of the corner of my eye as he passes through the house, especially when I'm really sad. He comes by to let me know he's still around and loves me. I say hi, and I feel the sparkle in the moment.

Twig was my best friend for 12 years before he had to leave. The more we love the more we grieve when we lose something we love. It's okay to be sad and angry and to forget things and cry and whatever else happens when you lose them. I love more and spread kindness now because maybe other people have lost someone they love—animal or human. I spend time in nature and watch the little critters of the forest. I watch for a Red Admiral butterfly fluttering by. And I smile when I feel like smiling, and I honor Twig's memory and all the others I have lost.

Chapter 20

I AM Bliss Buzzy Bee I AM
Wham-Bam-SHAZAAM!
By Timothy Stuetz

Bumble bees and honeybees,
  You surely do know,
Pollinating fruits, veggies 'n trees,
  From watermelon to mango.

Gourmet chefs of pollen and honey,
    Faithful servants of humanity.
Busily buzzing in their kitchen hive,
    Making foods to keep us all alive!

But more than food we all do need,
    To be nourished and inspired to succeed.

For that there is a special bee
    You may not now know.
A Queen Bee? No!
    Nor a nurse or guard bee!

A bee who hums hymns of harmony
    To help all life glow and grow
In vibrant health and unity,
    Serving our worldwide community!

A special bee who, while buzzing
    From flower to flower one day,
Buzzed bumpingly into a bear so loving,
    A bear from far, far, very far away.

The Great Bear Constellation his home,
    On Earth to spread love he does roam.

Dazed from this bump out of the blue,
    A whack with resounding rumble,
Our little bee did bumble,
    "Who are you?"

Radiating love everywhere
    From his magical heart all aglow
Came a bliss-FULL— "Hello,
    I AM Bliss Beary Bear.
And you, my little bee,
    Who might you be?"

"A simple bee am I.
    My name, Kauai (kah-WYE-ee).
I buzz from bud to bloom,
    Zoom-Zoom-ZOOM!

Never seen a bear like you,
    All aglow from head to toe,
Suddenly flying into you
    Was quite the blow!
Yet, I feel so alive and new,
    Tingling through and through!
Oh my, what did you do?"

"The tingling tingles are you,
    Your own bliss bubbling brew.
A bliss you too, like me, can share,
    Zoom-Zoom-ZOOMING through the air."

"I do feel buzzingly bee-lightful.
    Oh, so blissfully blissful!
A honey-sweet revival.
    To share a gift so ambrosial,
I would be forever grateful."

"Then a request I have of thee,
      Little bee named Kauai:
How would you like to be
      My special Bliss Beary Emissary?
A busy, buzzing blissful luminary,
      Inspiring all to be sweet as golden honey,
Co-creating *global harmony.*"

"Who me?
      I'm but a simple bee?"

"Yes, you surely be,
      A simple bee,
A humble bee,
      The perfect bee,
So ready and steady
      To fulfill your destiny!

Hollow, yet strong as bamboo,
      Empty of the ego's 'Self'Dom.
A bee I see so true, through and through,
      Able to embody the Divine KingDom."

"Yes, ever so ready I be,
      Oh, beloved Bliss Beary,
Though I know not what it means for me!"

"A different bee you will surely BE,
As that Me dissolves into WE!

That feeling so alive and new,
      That tingling through and through,
Will expand evermore and sprout a new You!

You'll pollinate people seeking to be free,
	With love, bliss and equality."

"BIZZY—BUZZY—BEEZZY,"
	Buzzed Kauai in the gentle breeze.
"What a *super-duper surprise*
	To gift people such a *pollen prize!*"

"Then look into my eyes so bright,
	Before you resume your flight.
A gift I will now bestow—
	So, you will forever know,
And be the Divine-flow!"

Gazing into Bliss Beary's eyes,
	Sparkling pools of love and light,
Kauai received a blessed surprise!
	A waterfall of glittering love and light
Flowed through her body as she took flight.

With wings whirling and twirling in ecstasy,
	Kauai embodied a precious new identity:
"I AM Bliss Buzzy Bee,
	Forever free to be Me.

I AM Bliss Buzzy Bee I AM,
Gentle as a baby lamb.

I AM Bliss Buzzy Bee,
Full of glee—Whoopee!

I AM Bliss Buzzy Bee I AM,
	Since into Bliss Beary Bear I did ram;
Wham-Bam-SHAZAAM!

I AM Bliss Buzzy Bee,
    Soul 'blissed' to be with thee.
And a Bliss Beary Bear Emissary
    You too can be,
By diving into my story
    From cover to cover,
Over and over.

I AM all that I AM,
    Appreciating all that LIVES.
I AM all that IS,
    Appreciating all that I AM.

I AM alert and so alive,
    Abuzz in a flower or around my hive.
Always asking 'What do I want to know?'
    I'm forever in life's Divine-flow.

I'M authentic, I AM me,
    Bliss Buzzy Bee.
A bizzy-buzzy-Beezzy Beauty,
    I AM Bliss, a Bliss Buzzy Bee!

I AM breathing and flying so freely,
    Like you, doing a cartwheel or wheelie.

I AM connected with the Great 'I AM,'
    Who says: 'It's never a scam
To declare, I AM That I AM!'

I AM always celebrating the I AM That is You,
    Hopeful everyone will do that too.

I AM cheerful and free to choose,
    Knowing I may win or lose.

I admit my mistakes,
    So, there will be no retakes.

Clean in mind and body,
    HEART 'n SOUL I embody.

I AM creative,
    Oh, what a natural 'stim-u-la-tive'!

I AM always looking for ways to compliment others,
    For all are my si'stars' and bro'star' brothers.

I'M content to be Bliss Buzzy Bee,
    Simply happy to be me.

Courageous with power,
    I explore hour after hour,
Wildflower upon wildflower,
    In sunshine or rain shower!

I AM not afraid to cry,
    Then fly, fly, fly,
Oh, so high, High, HIGH!

Soul confident I AM, hummingly seeking in wonder,
    Never looking to pillage or plunder.

I AM deLIGHT,
    Free of fright.

I AM desireless, yet full of dreams,
    And free of schemes.

I AM Bliss Buzzy Bee!
    I AM Me,
Buzzing with integrity.

I AM curious to discover,
    With bliss to uncover.

I AM happy to discuss,
    But adverse to make a fuss!

I AM Oh So Divine,
    My very own Shrine.

I AM in ecstasy when I dance, swing,
    And do my thing!

I AM free to disagree,
    While honoring another's opinion in equality.

I AM full of enthusiasm,
    Never depressed in a deep, dark chasm.

I AM fearless,
    But not tearless.

I AM Bliss Buzzy Bee I AM,
    Ever since Bliss Beary Bear
Awakened Me to Who I AM!
    Such a fortuitous bump I do declare,
Right out of the thin blue air!

I AM forgiving,
    A fulfilling way of living!
A friend,
    On whom you can depend.

I AM giving,
    Making me feel like dancing and singing.

I AM grateful,
    Never hateful.

I AM goodness.
    Count on that with sureness.

I AM living in and as grace,
    Regardless of time or place.

I AM GRRReat!
    Oh Yes, I AM First-RRRate!

Happy-Happy-HAPPY—
    A happy Bliss Buzzy Bee I truly BEE.

I AM humble,
    Even when I stumble, mumble, and bumble.

I AM healthy and choose healthy activities and foods,
    Which create happy, joyful, blissful moods.

I'M full of ideas and set my intentions,
    To fulfill them free of tensions and apprehensions.

I AM whirling in perpetual bliss,
  Even in stillness and illness.

I AM imagining each moment is unsurpassed,
  Much-Much-MUCH BETTER than the last,
For the past is past, Past-Past-PAST.
  Oh, What a BLAST!
Yes, over and done—PAST-PAST-PAST!

In tune with my intuition,
  Knowing it brings all to fruition.
I AM keenly insightful,
  Which I find quite delightful.

Setting my course with a compass of positive intentions,
  My attention pollinates them, free of pretensions.

I AM joy—oh boy!

I AM kind,
  To misery and misfortune, not blind.

Open to knowledge, but not bound by it,
  I also trust my wit!

I AM laughter,
  But not a very good actor.

I AM an interested listener,
  Therefore, an eager learner."

"Yes, my buzzingly beautiful earthly emissary!
    An eager learner and a great mentor,
Not a braggart nor self-proclaimed professor,
    You surely now be, Bliss Buzzy Bee."

"Bliss Beary Bear! Is that you I hear,
    But with my delighted eyes do not see?"

"Yes, oh yes, I AM ever near,
    And love to hear you claim in glee—
'I AM Bliss Buzzy Bee I AM!'"

"Yes, I AM Bliss Buzzy Bee I Am!

I AM Love!
    Above all else, I AM LOVE!
Magically magical,
    A miraculous miracle.

I AM attuned to the music of Creation,
    The *one-and-only* Nation.
Here NOW,
    To, and in each moment, I BOW.

I AM original,
    Therefore, never miserable.
ONE with All That IS,
    My life's one true biz.

I'M heartful and peaceful,
    Passports to blissful.
Ever optimistic,
    Never ever pessimistic!

I AM Bliss Buzzy Bee I AM!

I AM never ALONE.
    Like ET, I phoned HOME!

I AM passionate and present,
    And oh, so pleasant.
Open to your personal perspective,
    BUT NOT to your coercive objective.

I'M purposefully persistent,
    And consciously consistent.
Playful and prayerful,
    Faithful not doubtful.

I AM poetry in motion,
    Like waves in the ocean.
Always quiet internally,
    Amidst what's appearing externally.

I AM aware of the power of 'PLEASE'
    And too, 'I AM SORRY'
Never buzzing just to appease,
    Always humming from my heart's glory!

I AM cautiously open to risks frisky,
    But never risks exceedingly risky.

I'M a grateful receiver,
    And joyful giver.
Ever responsive,
    Never reactive.

I AM always on the ball,
    Respectful of all!
Soul sacred,
    I *know not* hatred.

I AM serene,
    Never sting to be mean!
Oh, so serene am I,
    A Yoda Jedi!

I AM Bliss Buzzy Bee,
    My body as tiny as a flea,
Compared to the immensity,
    Of my eternal soul's infinity!

I AM Bliss Buzzy Bee I AM.
    Soul I AM.
Soulful I AM.
    Soul-Luminous I AM.
So FULL I AM.

I AM, whether awake, asleep,
    Or in a dream so deep.

I'M a student of each moment,
    Ahh, so probingly potent.
Teeming in understanding,
    Never demanding.

I AM transparent,
    Patient and tolerant!
Thankful for ALL,
    My heart's protocol!

I AM in thankful awe,
    From sunrise to sunset,
AND FOR each sunrise and sunset;
    Divine art without flaw!

A truth-seeking sleuth,
    Living in truth,
I AM truthful,
    Never speaking bull.

An ocean of unconditional love,
    The peace of a dove,
I AM a unique miracle,
    Soul Uni-Verse-ALL!

I'M virtuous,
    Not righteous.
Always trying,
    Without striving or conniving.

I AM willing to willfully fulfill,
    Destiny's Divine Will.
Able to materialize,
    Ideas my heart creatively supplies.

I AM wise,
    Never in disguise.
Able to yield,
    Yet steadfast like a shield.

I AM a great pyramid of energy,
    Secreting *royal jelly majesty,*
Finding fun in all I do
    Whoo-Hoo!

I'M a fountain bubbling,
    Eternal youth erupting.
Beaming with ZEST,
    Oh, soul blessed!

I AM Zestful ZEAL,
    Not one to steal!

I AM Bliss Buzzy Bee
    And a blissful being
You too can be,
    By into my story diving,
From cover to cover,
    Over and over.

Yes, Blissful like me,
    You too will be,
A Bliss Beary Bear Emissary
    Just like me,
A *global luminary!*

I AM Bliss Buzzy Bee I AM,
    And I LOVE YOU!
I Soul Love You, I Do!
    Wham-Bam-SHAZAAM!"

Chapter 21

From Shy to Soaring
Cecilia's Flight to Confidence
By Eileen Poniński

Cecilia's Birthday: Age Eight

"Happy Birthday to you!"

The whole classroom burst into a chorus of cheerful singing. Cecilia's heart sank as all eyes faced toward her.

Her face turned as pale as the whiteboard, and her fluffy pink princess dress felt heavier with each passing note.

Why does everyone have to look at me?

Gina, dressed all in black, who was known for being mean, saw her chance. She leaned closer to Cecilia and whispered, just loud enough for her to hear,

"You look like a monkey,
and you smell like one too!"

Cecilia's humiliation deepened.

Why is this happening on my eighth birthday?

Tears welled up in her eyes, and she didn't say a word as she fled the classroom.

Always trying to please the teacher, Gina volunteered to bring Cecilia back. She found Cecilia leaning over the bathroom sink, her soft sobs echoing through the tiled space.

"You're such a baby, can't even handle a simple birthday song! What a loser!" Gina taunted, her cruel laughter echoing in the bathroom.

Cecilia desperately wanted to fight back, but her voice betrayed her. She stood there, defenseless, wiping her tears as Gina's words cut deeper. "Whatever, I don't care. Mrs. Coté wants you back in the classroom," Gina responded as she pushed her out the bathroom door and onto the floor.

Cecilia, unable to speak, nodded weakly as she rose to follow, a silent plea for the bullying to end.

Why can't I speak up?

Because of Gina's mean words, Cecilia chose to stay inside the strong, protective castle of complete silence.

Welcome to the Troop!

Weeks later, the parent-teacher conference carried an atmosphere of concern.

Mrs. Coté, with perfectly styled blonde hair, expressed it first by saying, "I know Cecilia is a shy girl, but she seems to have withdrawn since her birthday."

Cecilia's mom, fidgeting with her pink purse, confirmed she had observed the same, "Cecilia won't talk to anyone when we're out," she added in a worried tone.

Within the realm of shared worry, a delicate ray of hope emerged.

"Consider a Girl Scout troop?" proposed Mrs. Coté. "Elizabeth, her classmate, often talks about her troop's adventures with her mom as the leader. It might take Cecilia out of her silent cocoon."

Mrs Coté's words lingered in Cecilia's mom's mind. She was desperate to help her daughter, so before Cecilia could protest, they were already driving to the troop meeting.

"Have fun!" Cecilia's mom cautiously smiled as Cecilia got out of the car.

Before Ms. Dawn, the troop leader, could introduce herself, Cecilia was underneath a table, hiding.

"Hey girls, come sit around our new friend Cecilia!" suggested Ms. Dawn as she sat on the soft, rainbow floor.

Elizabeth, a bright, bubbly girl with wavy brown hair, sat next to Cecilia, as did Camila, a caring, outgoing, and talented girl with dark hair and sun-kissed skin who loved to sing.

"Hey! I recognize you from school! We're making flowers out of tissue paper! I'm so excited, how about you?" Elizabeth exclaimed, always eager to make more friends.

"I am!" Camila replies.

Cecilia looked up at them like a sad puppy and nodded.

Elizabeth's playful voice filled the air throughout the meeting as the troop created their paper bouquets.

Meetings were difficult for a long time. Cecilia wanted to speak and make friends, but she felt like a weed in a patch of flowers, not wanted and soon to be pulled.

"I like your dress! You look like a princess!" Elizabeth exclaimed at a troop meeting.

"Thank. . . you. . ." Cecilia quietly responds, her voice shaking.

"Do you like playing pretend?" Elizabeth asks in a holler. "I like to pretend I'm a baker, crafting delicious goodies!"

"You used to wear dresses all the time, Cecilia. What happened?"

"Gina was mean to me on my birthday," Cecilia quietly responds, tears welling up in her eyes.

"But I like pretending I'm a princess. Because if I was a princess, I might be able to speak bravely."

Friendship!

On the school playground, Cecilia and Elizabeth were swinging together when Gina approached, shouting in her usual sinister tone.

"CECILIA!

GET OFF!

THAT'S MY SWING!"

"No! She's playing with me. And we're not done," Elizabeth screamed back as Gina scurried off like a wounded rat.

I finally have a real friend! Cecilia thought to herself, her happiness now bubbling up from inside.

Later that day, at the end of the troop meeting, Elizabeth and Cecilia were stacking chairs in the corner of the room.

"Do you think we could have a sleepover?" Cecilia asked with twinkling eyes.

"Maybe. You would have to ask my mom, though. I asked her last week, but she said you need to talk to her before she would allow it," Elizabeth replied.

Cecilia took a deep breath and walked over to Elizabeth's mom. "Ms. Dawn? Can Elizabeth and I have a sleepover, please?" Cecilia quietly whispers, looking down with her thick brown hair over her face.

"Look into my eyes, sweetheart," she replied.

Cecilia repeated the question, looking at her without actually making eye contact.

"Good enough for me, dear. Yes, you can come and have a sleepover, but you have to promise to talk," Ms. Dawn says.

A couple of hours into the sleepover, the phone rang. Cecilia's mom picked it up with horrendous dread, expecting to have to pick up her daughter.

"OH MY GOSH, ANN! SHE WON'T STOP TALKING! I'VE NEVER HEARD HER SPEAK THIS MUCH!" Ms. Dawn exclaimed.

Cecilia's mom let out a sigh of relief. "What did you do to her?!"

"Haha!"

"I told you she talks a lot at home!" Cecilia's mom replied, snickering uncontrollably.

New Beginnings: Age Nine

"Hey, are you gonna join the Choir this year? It's really fun, and we get to perform in the talent show!" Camila excitedly asked Cecilia and Elizabeth as they walked into their bright new 4th-grade classroom.

Elizabeth immediately shouted, "I'm in!"

Cecilia reluctantly said, with a quiver in her voice, "I'll do it too."

With friends, it seemed the lightbulb of anxiety Cecilia had been carrying with her ever since her eighth birthday finally started to dim as she started to seek the spotlight.

After months of choir practice, the talent show finally arrived. After they sang, all three girls watched the other performances. One in particular caught Cecilia's eye the most. It was a girl wearing a purple unitard covered in rhinestones, performing on something called an aerial Lyra. She soared through the air, creating beautiful shapes with her body.

Wow, I want to do that!

As soon as Cecilia got home from the show that night, she looked up stretching routines online and found an aerial studio in her area.

Miss Brandi and Miss Rachel, the enchanting instructors at the aerial studio, extended a warm welcome to Cecilia as she stepped into the world of aerial arts.

Cecilia, wide-eyed with a mixture of excitement and nervousness, leaned in to share her concerns with Miss Brandi. With a comforting smile that reflected years of teaching experience, she whispered back, "You've got this, Cecilia. We're here to guide you every step of the way."

"Don't worry, Cecilia," Whispered Bre, a fellow student of the class who overheard, "They make it look scarier than it is. You'll love it here!" Her eyes gleamed with enthusiasm.

"Thanks, Bre, I'm kinda afraid of falling off," Cecilia responds nervously.

"They'll teach you the right way to do it!" says Bre with a wink and a smile.

The Performance: Age Eleven

After lots of practice, Cecilia was ready for the studio showcase!

"It's time! You're going to slay this, and I'm so proud of you!" Cecilia's Mom encouraged her backstage.

Cecilia could see her family and friends in the audience smiling brightly. She gave her mom a big hug and then walked out in her red sparkly outfit.

Nervously, she approaches the aerial silks.

Each move upon the silks is graceful as she hits each beat of the music, but doubt crept in as the finale drew closer—the big drop!

Although Cecilia practiced this dozens of times, the thought of her eighth birthday rushed in.

I'm not sure I can do this!

But then she looked at the audience and saw everyone she loved cheering her on.

Keep your toes pointed, posture high, and don't look down, she thought.

"You can do it!" her Aunt Lolly screamed at the top of her lungs. Her voice soothing Cecilia, pushing her to keep going. When Cecilia let go of the silks, she heard Lolly shriek in complete shock.

The crowd erupts into a round of applause.

"I can't believe I did that! It was really scary, but it felt awesome! And Aunt Lolly's reaction was hilarious!" she giggled as she shared her thrilling experience with her friends afterward.

Miss Brandi and Miss Rachel, with big smiles on their faces, came over. "You did amazing, Cecilia!" Miss Brandi said proudly.

Cecilia smiled at them, feeling proud of herself. "Thank you both for helping me be brave. I never thought I could do something like this."

"See, I told you it wasn't as scary as it seemed!" Bre added.

Cecilia's mom joined in, happiness in her eyes "I'm so proud of you, sweetie. You've come a long way, and I can't wait to see where your confidence takes you."

Cecilia gave her mom a tight hug, grateful for all the support that had helped her find her voice and courage. As she looked at her friends and instructors, she realized that she was no longer the quiet girl who had been bullied.

She was now a brave and determined kid, ready to face new challenges.

Chapter 22

Secrets of the Weeping Willow
By Carrie Freshour

Spring

Under the afternoon sun, my backyard transformed into a canvas of golden hues. Spring's embrace graced the weeping willow, dressed in cascading emerald strands. Its delicate branches unfurled with joy, mirroring nature's teardrops in a mesmerizing dance of vibrant green.

I lugged my pink suitcase and *that* old patchwork blanket, the only one Mom allowed outside. I set them down briefly and pulled the sliding glass door shut. *THUMP*. With determined grunts, I pulled my treasures off the wooden deck and headed straight to my hideout, hidden under the thick, sprawling branches of the weeping willow that swept the ground below, making it feel like a new world.

My pink suitcase, a mobile universe of dolls and tiny outfits, took center stage.

The rusty-colored blanket, worn but cherished, unfolded under the embrace of the weeping willow.

I heard her unmistakable presence before I saw her. It was Alex, my bestie since forever. A perfectly fine gate sits between her yard and mine, yet she insists on clambering over the fence.

As Alex lands just outside the reach of the drooping branches, her canery yellow all-stars signal another day filled with laughter and make-believe adventures.

"Hey, Alex!" I called.

She sighed heavily.

"Babies are the worst!" she exclaimed. "They're tiny, always crying, and steal all the attention!"

"Yeah, I bet my parents will forget my name once the baby arrives," I said.

"Well, my parents still remember mine. 'Alex, get the bottle. Alex, get a diaper.' Ugh," she sighed.

Chuckling, I added, "I've got a few months before my brother arrives. Let's not talk about babies!"

Our laughter rings out under the protection of the weeping willow, momentarily casting aside the budding concerns that would soon darken our innocent world.

"I love hanging out with you, Alex. You're just the best. You make even baby rants fun," I smiled, gathering my dolls and folding that old blanket.

As we leave our secret haven, Alex yells, "Hey, my cousins are coming over Sunday for the family BBQ; Shane's a riot; you'll love him. He is in *high school* and just got his license, so maybe he will take us for a ride!"

"SOUNDS FUN!" I holler as Alex catapulted over her fence.

Summer

Alex's cousin Shane started showing up more often in the following weeks. It wasn't a big deal at first. He had just gotten his driver's license, and the freedom seemed to bring him our way.

Sometimes, our moms let him drive us to the ice cream shop, and he'd let us listen to our favorite songs. There was an excitement in the air, a sense of adventure that made our afternoons feel like mini road trips.

Shane wasn't as playful as Alex, but he had a way of making me feel special. He'd listen to my stories, even the silly ones about my dolls.

In the sun-soaked days of summer, Shane's wheels and high school tales added excitement to our willow tree adventures. Making me feel like I was part of the grown-up world.

It was an unexpected friendship, one that seemed harmless at the time. Little did I know, this connection was on the verge of transforming, much like the lush curtain of green branches shifting into greenish-brown strands with the changing seasons.

Fall

As fall approached and fith grade loomed, the once vibrant weeping willow tree began shedding its leaves. Our tales shifted from carefree laughter to a whispering concern, hinting at changes beyond the golden days of summer.

One day, as Alex was busy with lacrosse, Shane appeared unexpectedly.

"Just you and me this time?" he said, suggesting an ice cream run.

It sounded like fun, but this time, my tummy felt different. The butterflies, once fluttering with excitement, started turning into buzzing bees. Something felt off, but I couldn't quite grasp it.

"Oh, I can't today, sorry," I stammered, feeling like a complete loser.

"Come on, Sarah, we won't be gone long, and no one will know! It will be our secret."

Shane started a tickle attack on me; I giggled, but it didn't feel funny.

I just want to leave.

I got up to go, covered by the weeping willow. Suddenly, my heart raced, and I felt a panic. I needed to get inside my house.

Trying to calm this weird feeling inside me, I aimlessly rubbed the corners of my blanket, an old habit that soothed me.

"I, uh, have soccer practice. I just came outside for a few minutes but realized I must get going. I heard my mom calling just as you showed up!"

In the weeks that followed, Shane's boundary-pushing continued. He showed up under the willow like he had a radar for the exact moment I stepped through those branches, hidden from everyone's view.

Hugs and tickles persisted, and Alex's silent observation became more noticeable.

Despite my discomfort, I didn't know how to address it.

Once a haven, the willow tree felt distant, dark, and sad, like the once bright emerald green strands falling swiftly.

Then, a turning point.

I remember Mrs. Susan, the school counselor, shared a story about listening to our bodies: "Your body has a special voice called an instinct," she read. "It's like your own compass, helping you when you feel something inside."

Her words resonated like echoes in a canyon, tapping into a part of me I couldn't express. "When you feel something inside, it's guiding you through your world, keeping you safe," she had read.

Suddenly, it hit me! Something felt wrong about Shane.

Winter

Yearning for guidance, I tried talking to my mom, but the topic of the coming baby dominated our conversations lately, making me uneasy.

The icky feeling lingered until one day, after another insightful story time with Mrs. Susan, I found the courage to open up to my mom—*I will demand her attention,* I thought, *at a time when she can't resist it!*

Later that night, as Mom was taking her nightly bath, I snuck in. Shielding my eyes, partly so I wouldn't have to see her and maybe a bit so she wouldn't see me either, I drew in a deep breath.

"I don't like babies, and I don't like boys; how will I ever like this little brother!" I confessed.

My mom chuckled warmly, "Clearly, you sought me out while I was in the bath. Is there something on your mind, Sarah?

Peeking through my fingers, I caught a glimpse of Mom looking at me and her expanding belly. Gathering courage, I blurted out, "Shane makes me feel funny, and I don't like it when he tickles me!"

Feeling a wave of embarrassment, I covered my face with my hands, and then, making matters worse, tears started streaming down like a waterfall.

Amidst the quiet that felt like an eternity, Mom didn't utter a word. But as I stole glances through my fingers, I saw her wrapping herself in a robe and kneeling before me. She simply hugged me.

Still, she didn't say a thing. It was both comforting and unnerving.

Was she angry? But then, she's hugging me, so maybe she can't be that mad.

Thoughts swirled in my head, making it all the more terrifying.

Finally, breaking the silence, Mom gently pulled back, her eyes filled with warmth and concern.

"Sarah," she began softly, "I'm relieved you came to talk to me about this. Sharing your feelings is important, especially if something makes you uncomfortable. I'm always here to support you.

Can you tell me more about how Shane's making you feel and why it's bothering you?" she asked.

"I remember a story Mrs. Susan read in class," I began. "It talked about this inner compass that guides us when something feels wrong. I, um, feel like my compass is trying to tell me something, but I can't quite figure it out. If I don't soon, I might lose my best friend."

Mom listened intently as I unraveled the story of Shane's increasing presence under the willow tree.

"Thank you for trusting me, my brave girl," Mom embraced me. "Your courage is admirable, and I'm here for you, always— even when I seem distracted. We'll navigate this together." Her voice was gentle as a breeze, skillfully diffusing the tension in my heart.

"I'm embarrassed," I admitted, my voice quivering, "but I don't know why." A single tear trailed down my cheek.

"Trusting your instincts, as Mrs. Susan taught, shows incredible courage," Mom said warmly. "You have no reason to be ashamed; you have done nothing wrong," she reassured.

"I'm kinda puzzled about one part," I explained. "Mrs. Susan said, 'Sometimes, people can be kind—charming even. They seem helpful,' which is really confusing because that is similar to a friend's behavior?"

"What I can tell you," Mom replied, "is that most people mean well, but if your instincts—that voice inside you, is telling you something feels wrong, talking to an adult you trust is just the right thing to do! You did the right thing by coming to me."

Talking with my mom went way better than expected; she made the icky feeling melt like snow and showed me how to acknowledge my instincts and take meaningful action.

Spring

As the days unfolded, I uncovered the power in my voice, a force as significant as the whispering leaves beneath the willow tree.

Seeking clarity about Shane's behavior, my mom and I turned to the school counselor. With empathetic ears, she guided us, unraveling the uncomfortable tangle.

Empowered by her support, my mom, Alex's family, and I started addressing the tricky parts, mending the frayed edges of our friendship.

Mom beamed, "Your instincts will make you an amazing big sister; I trust you to share if something feels off."

Making a pact to always discuss our feelings, even amid the baby's arrival, reinforced our connection.

Alex, too, sensed Shane's unsettling presence. In our shared discomfort, we realized that open communication was key. Alex thought I wanted Shane as my friend, not realizing its impact on both of us.

Like the weeping willow strands thickening into a vibrant green, our friendship blossomed back to its usual vibrant self. Though worn and a bit torn, its comforting embrace continued to shield us from lingering discomfort like the tattered blanket symbolizing resilience.

Trusting our internal compass, our instincts guided us through uncertainty. Our moms and the school counselor, our steadfast allies, all helped us understand and protected us. We learned that sharing uneasy feelings with trusted adults is not only okay but a courageous step towards safety and well-being.

Dear reader,

As a survivor of childhood sexual abuse and a Mama, I write for all the brave souls reading. This is a powerful prevention story about grooming—a process that preys on innocence. Recognizing the signs is crucial. Trust your instincts; sudden gifts, excessive attention, or secretive behavior may be red flags. Through awareness and understanding, we can prevent.

For national support, contact organizations like the National Child Abuse Hotline.

Let's empower and protect the hearts of the little ones who depend on us.

With strength and resilience,

Carrie.

Chapter 23

The Great Green Magic Tractor
A Journey to the Roots of Africa
By Cedric Nwafor

Once upon a time, in a blossoming African community where the sun kissed the earth with warmth, and the fields stretched far and wide, children played freely, their laughter echoing through the air. In this land of plenty, the kids found a new game using food as their playthings, tossing fruits like balls and building forts with vegetables.

Babu, usually a beacon of gentle wisdom, watched this scene with a furrowed brow. His reaction was severe, unlike anything his granddaughter Dihari and her friends had ever seen.

"Why is Babu so upset?" they whispered among themselves, never having seen him in such a state.

Gathering the children under the great Baobab tree, Babu cleared his throat, his voice carrying the weight of many untold stories.

"Let me tell you a tale," he began, "of how we came to this point of abundance and the dangers that still lurk ahead."

He spoke of a time not too distant, in a small remote village, where despite toiling from dawn till dusk, the bellies of its people were never full.

"I remember those days like it was yesterday," Babu said, with his eyes looking out into the distance. "The gnawing hunger, the sacrifices we made, the regretful things we did.

Nami, a young boy from this very village, was in a constant battle against hunger, often eating scraps for pigs," Babu narrated. "This lack of food was not just a pang in his stomach but the root of many hardships that plagued the village. It bred a cycle of despair, casting gloom over their daily lives. Hunger brought the worst in people, even out of Nami.

However, Nami's life changed when he met visitors from a strange land who showed him wonders beyond his imagination. They invited him to see how they worked their lands. He was scared to leave everything he knew. A villager told him not to leave because it was a dangerous world out there. They reminded him of stories of those who left and never came back.

Nami was scared. He was about to say no to the visitors, but his father's words and reassurance gave him courage: 'What would life be if we had no courage to attempt and try new things? I know you are scared, but fear is a story we tell ourselves, a shadow in the corners of our courage, waiting to be illuminated by the light of our brave hearts.' With those words, Nami decided to follow the visitors.

Nami prepared for his journey to the visitors' land with a mix of excitement and nervousness. Each morning, as the sun crept over the horizon, he rose early, practicing the few words he had learned from the visitors, his tongue stumbling over the unfamiliar sounds. He gathered a small bundle of his belongings, wrapping them in a cloth his mother had woven. Inside, he placed a cherished photograph of his family, a handful of seeds from their garden, and a small, handmade toy that had been his constant companion since childhood.

Nami also spent hours with the village elders, absorbing their wisdom and stories about the world beyond their fields. Every night, under the starlit sky, he lay awake, envisioning the wonders he might see and the knowledge he could bring back to transform their village forever.

In this new land, Nami found himself amidst marvels beyond his wildest dreams, with one particular wonder capturing his awe—a green machine, a miracle of technology that defied all he knew. It stood there, majestic and powerful, a magnificent green beast humming with life. This contraption, with its whirring gears and gleaming metal, could transform barren earth into a tapestry of fertile soil in mere moments. It was unlike anything he'd ever seen—a magnificent green beast that could turn barren land into fertile ground in no time.

This machine, with its rhythmic hum and intricate parts, performed the work of many hands in a fraction of the time. It was Nami's hope, his chance for his village to break free from the shackles of hunger. The realization dawned on him that the amount of time this machine took to till the soil for five minutes was equivalent to the total amount of work his entire family could accomplish in a week. This wasn't just a tool; it was a symbol of a new era, a promise of a future where their community could thrive beyond the constraints of their past struggles.

In an incredible act of kindness, the visitors offered one of the green machines to Nami to take back with him. They had just one condition: the machine should never pick up rust; if so, they would take it back from Nami.

In the village square, Nami unveiled the *magic machine*, his eyes alight with hope.

Villagers gathered their faces a mix of intrigue and doubt. While some saw the machine as a beacon of progress and food security, others worried about its impact on traditional farming and their heritage. Elders debated, balancing the benefits of technology with the preservation of ancestral practices. Amidst these divided opinions, Nami realized his task was not just to fight hunger but to harmonize old ways with innovations for a sustainable future. However, as discussions continued, the machine stood unused for months upon months.

Nami leaned against the wall of his hut, gazing at the magic machine now covered in a thin layer of rust. He sighed, feeling the weight of his unfulfilled dreams. 'So much potential,' he murmured to himself, 'yet here it sits, unused.

One sunny morning, the visitors who brought the machine returned. Finding it untouched, they approached Nami. 'It's not just about the machine,' one of them said gently. 'It's about understanding and working with your people, blending old wisdom with new ideas. The real magic lies in the community's willingness to embrace change.'

These words echoed in Nami's mind as he walked to the elder meeting. Standing before the village elders, Nami's voice was clear and steady. 'Respected elders, I've reflected on your concerns and our traditions. I propose a compromise: Let me find just ten volunteers to test the machine in our fields. If I can't, I promise to return it. This is about finding a middle ground, where tradition and innovation can coexist for the betterment of our community.'

Nami continued, emphasizing his commitment to their well-being and traditions, 'If the volunteers find no benefit, or if the machine harms our land in any way, I will immediately stop the project and return to our traditional methods.'

The elders exchanged thoughtful glances, recognizing the sincerity in Nami's words and his respect for their wisdom. After a moment of deliberation, they nodded in agreement, accepting Nami's proposal as a balanced approach that respected both the potential of new technology and the importance of their ancestral practices.

Nami set out with a heart full of hope, determined to find the ten volunteers who would join him in this groundbreaking venture. He approached his fellow villagers, one by one, sharing his vision of how the magic machine could potentially transform their agricultural practices and ease their daily toil. However, his enthusiasm was met with skepticism and hesitation. Many farmers, deeply rooted in their traditional ways, were reluctant to risk the health of their land and crops on an unproven technology. They politely, yet firmly, declined his offer, fearing the unknown consequences of such a drastic change in their farming methods.

Despite these initial setbacks, Nami's spirit remained unbroken. He understood their fears, knowing that change was often daunting and met with resistance, but he also believed in the promise of progress and the benefits it could bring to their community. With patient determination, he continued his quest, hoping to find those few who were willing to embrace the possibility of a brighter future. His resolve never wavered as he tirelessly sought out those willing to step forward with him into this new era of farming, confident that his efforts would eventually bear fruit.

Nami's persistence eventually paid off. After many days of conversations and gentle persuasion, he finally found the ten farmers he needed. These were individuals who, despite their initial apprehensions, were moved by Nami's passion and the potential to improve their lives. They were a diverse group, some young and eager for change, others more experienced and curious about the new possibilities. Each shared a common trait: a spark of courage to venture into the unknown. With this small yet brave group assembled, Nami felt a renewed sense of hope and excitement. They were ready to embark on this experimental journey together, opening a new chapter in the village's history, one that promised to blend the wisdom of the past with the innovations of the future.

The experiment of the ten daring farmers resulted in a harvest that was nothing short of miraculous. As the season progressed, the fields cultivated with the aid of the magic machine flourished beyond anyone's expectations. The crops grew robust and healthy, reaching heights and yields that were unprecedented in the village's history.

When harvest time arrived, the farmers were astounded by the abundance they had reaped. Their granaries overflowed with grains, and their vegetable patches were a mosaic of vibrant colors and bountiful produce. This extraordinary harvest was more than enough to feed the entire village, with plenty to spare. The success of these ten farmers became a testament to the potential of embracing new methods, and it sparked a sense of wonder and possibility throughout the community. Their courage to try had not only transformed their own lives but had also sown the seeds of change and prosperity for the entire village.

As word of their bountiful yield spread, the initial skepticism that had clouded the community's perception of the magic machine began to dissipate. By the following year, every farmer in the village was eager to adopt this new method, inspired by the tangible benefits they had witnessed. The once hesitant voices were now filled with enthusiasm, ready to embrace the blend of tradition and innovation.

Amidst this wave of change, Nami shared a reflective insight, 'This machine, as powerful as it is, could destroy our soil just as easily as it has given us a bountiful harvest. It's merely a tool capable of both good and harm. The real magic doesn't reside in the machine; it's in us, in the richness of our soils, the resilience of our seeds, and the decades of wisdom we've nurtured in harmony with the land. Our true strength lies in how we use this tool, blending it with our knowledge and respect for the earth.' Nami's words echoed a profound truth, reminding the village that while technology could aid their efforts, the essence of their success lay in their heritage and their symbiotic relationship with nature."

Babu's voice softened. "I apologize for my severe reaction. You didn't know the days of hunger. But remember, if we don't appreciate what we have, we can easily lose it."

Dihari's eyes widen with curiosity. She turned to her mom, who had been listening quietly to the storytelling session. "Mom, where is Nami now? Is he still around?" she asked eagerly.

Her mom smiled softly, a twinkle in her eye, and replied, "Dihari, Nami is closer than you think. Nami is your Babu. All this time, he's been sharing his own story with us."

A chorus of gasps and surprised murmurs rippled through the group of children. They looked at their Babu with newfound admiration and awe. One of the kids exclaimed, "Wow, so Babu is the hero of this amazing story!"

Another child chimed in, her voice resolute, "I'll never waste food again, knowing what Babu went through!"

Inspired and proud, Dihari declared, "I want to be just like Babu. I'll respect the soil, help reduce waste, and make sure our village never goes hungry again." Her words echoed the determination and spirit of her grandfather, signaling a new generation ready to uphold and build upon the legacy of harmony, sustainability, and respect for the earth.

As the sun set, casting golden hues over the village, the children, led by Dihari, returned home, their hearts filled with tales of courage, wisdom, and the magic within.

Chapter 24

Namati's Return Home
From Serpent to Dragon
By N. S. Shakti

It's time to open your eyes.

These words floated outside time and space, hanging in the between, echoing in the darkness and fading to a whisper. . . then nothing.

Namati opened her eyes, and there was still nothing.

She uncoiled herself and slowly emerged from the eggshell into the smooth darkness of the earth. She felt her sisters squirming all around her.

"Please stay!" She called to them blindly as they each slithered upon their own paths.

Genetically, Namati was identical to her mother, sisters, all their grandmothers, and great-grandmothers of time gone and to those yet to come. But something inside of her knew she was different, that she didn't belong, not really.

Namati had a fire in her belly and an incredible urge to break out from under the earth and fly high into the sky.

In reality, Namati was born into the blind snake family. She didn't know how she knew what she knew. She just knew a lot of things. It was what you would call her instincts.

Food! I sure am hungry!

In the farthest chamber of an abandoned ant colony, protected by a labyrinth of tunnels, was where Namati's mother had chosen to safely lay her precious clutch of eggs. Once done, she left, and they hatched themselves.

Can you imagine a baby being born needing no parents for protection, sustenance, guidance, nurturing, or love? The power of genetic coding and wisdom that exists within these miraculous creatures at birth? To protect oneself, grow up, and survive all by yourself?

The ant colony was indeed totally abandoned by the ants, with not one egg to be found! Namati was a little disappointed that all her exploring had been in vain.

But she was brave.

So, she left the safety of the colony and began to gently nudge her way through the soft, warm earth.

Bump!

She knew a lot of things; what she didn't know was what this roundish obstacle was in her path. It wasn't food! At least not her kind of food. She was searching for eggs, ant eggs, termite eggs, or pupae. Yummy! But this was rough, bumpy, and quite large, with roots extending and intertwining into the earth.

What is this?

Namati's thoughts were interrupted by beautiful sounds floating down through the earth from above.

"Snowflakes on daffodils and whispers through seasons . . ."

Allyssa, an earth spirit, hummed a song she had once heard as she tended to dying daffodils. She was an Alfrar, belonging to the Huddenfolk of Iceland. You probably know them as elves. These magical creatures are caretakers of the one constant in nature—change. Whenever any living being, anywhere in the cosmos, is in transition, transformation, rebirth, or resurrection, all their spirit has to do is call.

A call from the soul to these earth spirits summons them, and they are happy to help in any way needed.

Namati didn't know any of this, but she was shy, so she froze behind the daffodil bulb, buried deep in the earth, hidden out of sight.

Above ground, Allyssa stopped singing to greet a friend.

"Oh, hello, Caterpillar! You don't seem yourself this morning! Are you quite alright?"

"Morning Allyssa. Your daffodils are dying, and I feel so am I," sighed Caterpillar sadly.

"I know just the spot for you where you could settle yourself, spin a cozy cocoon, and snuggle down for a nice long nap, I don't think it's dying that's ailing you!"

"Not dying? A nap, you say?"

"Yes! Naps are very powerful things. They help us conserve energy needed to live life, transform, and, in your case, for metamorphosis!"

"Meta-what now?"

"Errr, you know you are a butterfly, right?"

"Hahaha hahaha! I'm a grub!" Caterpillar sputtered over its laughter.

"Yes, yes, that you are *now,* but in reality, you're a butterfly who will break out from your cocoon with delicate wings of wondrous colors, and you will live among the flowers, sip on their nectar, and fly!"

Both Namati, inside the earth, and Caterpillar outside, were mesmerized by Allyssa's words.

There are some things you know, thought Namati, *and some that you learn!*

Namati inched away; she needed food first! Then, she was going to find out more about this metamorphosis business. She wanted wings to fly, too!

Her search led her outside, where she was further blinded by the mid-day sun.

EEK! I don't like this!

Darting across the grass, she hid under a pile of leaves. Once calm, she sensed an ant hill nearby. She squirted out some poo and then some special clear ant-repelling liquid and rolled and wriggled her way through this mixture a couple of times.

This shield would allow her to eat in peace; she was not in the mood for a speedy gobble fest.

She dove into an ant hill, slithering deep into the nest, and found a stash of eggs. She feasted to her heart's content and, on the way out, grabbed some pupae too! Namati was the brightest, happiest blind snake on the planet!

Nap time!

Hey! Maybe when I wake up, I will have wings!

Namati rested under a pile of rocks.

In her dream, she was flying! She was an agile viper, a clever rattlesnake, a mighty king cobra.

When she awoke, she was just Namati.

Her light flickered and dimmed. She couldn't see like other snakes could. She wasn't mighty or majestic, fearsome or wise. She was just a snake, the smallest of them all; she could even be considered a worm.

And there was no meta-mor. . .what was that word?

Disheartened, Namati suddenly missed her sisters. Although snakes are created to be independent and solitary, blind snakes can be social creatures.

Namati returned home to find all her sisters curled up together. When she joined them, they excitedly shared stories of their adventures.

"I found termites, raced in, ate the eggs super-fast, and dashed right out."

"I narrowly escaped being scooped up and carried away in a flower pot!"

"I learned about meta-mor-umm. . .metamorphosis," Namati shared proudly.

Her sisters were very curious about this important-sounding word.

"What does it mean? Metamorphosis?"

"Rest and transformation. And then we can fly!"

"Really? I don't think so! Snakes grow and shed skin so we can grow some more," said one of her blind sisters.

"Wings? Snakes don't fly!" said another sister.

Namati felt her excitement disappear, and her light dimmed again, as she began to doubt the magic of metamorphosis. Maybe her sisters were right?

But she wanted to fly! Deep down inside, that felt right.

One morning, she woke up very uncomfortable. She had this urge to rub her face on a rock, and her body was very tight.

Metamorphosis!

She squirmed forward eagerly, shedding her skin. It fell off in bits and pieces—a trail of rubbery rings. And no wings!

She was super disappointed.

I was so sure I was ready to transform!

Namati roamed deep inside the earth, aimlessly burrowing this way and that. Eventually, she found herself in the underground bed of daffodil bulbs.

Allyssa was bustling about. She saw Namati, and a surge of excitement ran through her as she immediately recognized the soul in front of her.

"Hello! I'm Allyssa!" she said brightly. Her musical voice was familiar to Namati.

Shyly, she replied, "Hi! I am Namati. I love your voice; my light brightens whenever I hear it."

"That's so sweet. Have we met?"

"Oh no, but I've heard you singing, and I also overheard you talking to Caterpillar! You know, this metamorphosis stuff is confusing me. What am I?"

Allyssa saw Namati's light flickering as she spoke.

"Namati, metamorphosis is built into your soul and is different for everyone. When your light is bright and shining steadily, not changing with situations, thoughts, or feelings, that will be your moment of transformation."

"We all have a unique purpose that we may not be able to see. Once you realize you're an important part of the whole fabric of time, you will expand, grow wings, and fly."

"I don't understand," replied Namati glumly.

"You are a dragon," said Allyssa gently, "The missing piece. Destined to complete the Mighty Dragon Baby."

"A dragon? Woah! How does a tiny serpent like me become a dragon? Are you sure?"

"I know this as surely as I know that Caterpillar is a butterfly! Let me tell you the origin story."

"Before the beginning of time, the Great Dragon Mother laid an egg.

Within this magical egg is the entire cosmos.

Brother universes and sister universes.

Infinite galaxies and microscopic ones.

Humongous celestial bodies and tiny ones like the blue speck known as the planet Earth.

Stars that are suns to solar systems and planets that are moons to others.

Floating, raggedy rocks and smooth, polished ones.

Milky ways and black holes.

The dance of creation swirls and twirls inside the egg.

When the last fractal finds its way, the Mighty Dragon Baby will be complete and ready to be birthed.

That fractal, Namati, is you. Shine brightly, little one. Once you find your wings, fly deep down to the molten core of the earth. For there, the Great Dragon Mother awaits your arrival so her precious dragon baby can finally be born."

"Waiting for me?!" Namati gently hissed.

At the thought of this, everything she had always known: the feeling of not belonging, of knowing she was meant to be more than a serpent, that she was different than the others—she knew she could fly and see! It all suddenly made sense. She was destined for more.

With this awareness, she had a choice—was she a tiny serpent bound to earth? Or a magical dragon flying high, meant for an epic destiny?

She chose the magic. With a deep breath, she took a leap of faith—to believe in herself.

Her light began to shine brightly. The brighter it shone, the steadier it became.

Namati's belly was burning hot, and fire burst out of her, forming magnificent wings of glorious red and dazzling gold. She screeched with joy, launching herself high into the sky.

Somersaulting, she dove back towards Earth; just when it seemed she would crash, magically, the earth opened, giving way and welcoming her as if it had been waiting for this exact moment.

Through familiar tunnels, Namati now flew. Then deeper down, through new pathways, straight to the very center of the Earth.

What guided her? Her instincts or something more? Nothing mattered; all she knew was that she was being called home. So, she flew down, down, down.

Almost there, she spotted The Great Dragon Mother, glowing with colors the human eye is yet to see, perched atop a magnificent tree surrounded by flowing rivers of molten rock. It was the center of the Earth.

"Mother!" Namati's soul cried out.

Mother Dragon looked up and, seeing Namati, roared just one word upon her fiery breath, "Tathastu!"

Nestled among the roots of the tree rested the dragon egg. It began to crack, and everything went dark for Namati.

It's time to open your eyes.

Namati opened her eyes and saw The Everything!

When The Great Dragon Mother had roared, "Let it be done," in the ancient Indian tongue, "*Tathastu!*" the final fractal clicked into place. Namati became the eyes with keen sight for the Mighty Dragon Baby, just born.

You see dear child, no matter how great or small, we all have a very important part to play in this life and across time and space. Shine on brightly, dear one, for there is magic in you.

Chapter 25

An Introduction to Child White Dragon and Her Sisters

By K.J. Kaschula

CHILD WHITE DRAGON

Child White Dragon is what is known as an enigma—something or someone who is very mysterious and who is difficult to understand.

This particular dragon who embodies what is known as white light, the purest of all lights and energies, came to me during a time in my life when I needed her[1] the most—when the winds were changing direction and the life that I had come to know would change forever.

Child White Dragon became my metamorphosis, and I, in turn, her transformation. Her story came to me in bits and pieces. A tail swing over here, a flap of a wing over there, and a whisper from within. Her story, much like puzzle pieces, needed to be put together, and much like a puzzle required great time and great patience to figure out.

It is only now, with the publication of *Brave Kids: Short Stories to Inspire Our Future World-Changers, Volume 2,* that her final piece of the puzzle has been realized.

Child White Dragon is: our past, present, and future. She is also our protector, our guardian, and our own transformation. In some magical way she is us, all of us scattered across time, space, and dimensions.

There is one thing that she does ask of you, dear Big Human Bean and dear Little Human Bean—our HMS Explorer passengers, and that is to understand that her story, too, is forever changing or *evolving* within you, and that it takes great time and great patience to completely understand the magic of why her story came to you when it did. For stories, dear Passenger have a strange way of entering our lives at precisely the right moment in time.

---

1   Child White Dragon is a very unique character and may appear to you, dear Passenger as a he or a she. It is up to you to decide how this protector and guardian of the In-Between is perceived.

Once Child White Dragon's story has been read to you or by you, and some kind of knowledge or understanding has come from it, and of course, has been forgotten through time—then when you need her and her story the most, she along with her sisters will return to your bookshelf.

It is my hope, dear Big Human Bean and dear Little Human Bean, that every time you read her story, it sparks something new within you, some sort of understanding of your own life, of your own living, and the life you will or have lived.

HER SISTERS

The magic that unites us all has a strange way of making itself known to those who are watching and to those who are listening.

When I began writing for *Brave Kids, Vol. 2,* I knew that I wanted to write about a dragon, and I knew exactly which dragon I wanted to write about, although I knew not her name or her story. I only knew that I processed certain puzzle pieces of various shapes and sizes and that in order to realize her story, I needed to put them together. This, too, took great time and patience and went through many drafts before I got to the story told in this book.

With Child White Dragon's story complete, it now formed its own puzzle piece, and like a *Brave Kids* puzzle that needed to be put together, I was still missing two very important puzzle pieces. . .

The first puzzle piece: While gathering the 24 *Brave Kids, Vol. 2* authors, I came to the realization that I would like to end this volume the same way I began it—with a dragon. This dragon story became my *ouroboros*, a symbol of a serpent or, in this case, a dragon swallowing its tail. This symbol, much like the story of 'Child White Dragon,' represents rebirth as well as metamorphosis or transformation. It also represents connection—connecting us to one another, as well as connecting the magical spiritual world with the real world we *all* are currently living in.

The second puzzle piece: I was quite surprised when a third dragon entered the world of *Brave Kids*. She appeared just like her sister dragon—embodying the *ouroboros*; that being said, 'Child White Dragon' became *Brave Kids, Vol. 2's* start, and the third dragon story to enter this collection became its end.

Three dragons. Three stories. Three different and unique tellings of transformation and the crossing of the threshold into a new world, a new beginning.

Child White Dragon, Emmy the Dragon, and Namati, who transforms from a serpent to a dragon, helped me complete the *Brave Kids, Vol. 2* puzzle and opened my eyes further to the beauty of not only my own story but the stories of all 24 authors.

The last puzzle piece—the year of the dragon: The final piece to one's puzzle is not the finding of the last puzzle piece itself or the placing of that particular puzzle piece within its specific spot. It is dear passenger, the art of standing back and admiring its whole. Observing the full beauty of your great time spent and your great patience offered. While observing this beauty, I was offered the last piece to this grand designed puzzle, which allowed me to stand back in complete awe: 2024, the publication of

Brave Kids: Short Stories to Inspire Our Future World-Changers, Volume 2, is also the year of the dragon, in fact, it is a wood dragon, a dragon known to be full of energy and a dream of changing the world.

The mystical forces that brought these three dragons together, these three stories and these three different tellings, is truly a magic that unites us all and can only be understood though great time and great patience.

past. present. future.

The End.

Meet the
Brave Kids Authors

POSTCARDS OF BRAVERY

K.J. Kaschula
Children's Book Author,
Illustrator & Publisher
Chapter 1

The brave heroine of this tale, a Ms. **K.J. Kaschula,** is a children's book author, illustrator, book designer and Brave Kids Books Publishing Director. She's the creator of *The-Super-Dooper-Secret-Collection,* a series of books following the secret adventures of Little Lizzie who encounters the mystical, magical, and marvelous worlds never before seen by kid-kind until now! Discovery of Little Lizzie's first adventures can be found in *I Caught One of Santa's Reindeer,* and *I Captured the Easter Bunny's Chicken.* K.J. is also the mastermind behind *Brave Kids: Short Stories to Inspire Our Future World-Changers.*

K.J. or Kelly as she is known by, grew up in Gauteng, South Africa (her first home), where she found herself gravitating toward the arts of storytelling¬—her exploration: the field of motion picture!

When K.J. is not playing with stories, she's most likely tasting delicious dishes or sipping coffee in a café in Paris, France (her second home) or in her little town in South Africa.

Connect with **K.J. Kaschula** at: https://www.kjkaschula.com/

POSTCARDS OF BRAVERY

Susan Ernst

Chapter 2

Susan Ernst grew up in Mill Valley, California, and recently relocated to Chevy Chase, Maryland, to be closer to family. She is the proud mom of two successful daughters, Laura and Alissa. She has two amazing grandchildren.

Volunteer work in Cambodia motivated her to write children's stories. Over a period of about five years, Susan accompanied heart-centered volunteers who served children at a rescue center led by Agape International Missions (AIM). This nonprofit organization works to rescue, heal, and empower survivors of trafficking. Her heart broke for those kids, and she vowed to do whatever she could to help them have hope and to be brave!

Susan's first story can be found in *Brave Kids: Short Stories to Inspire Our Future World Changers, Vol I.* Chapter 20: "Chann is Called to the Principal's Office: A Change of Heart Can Help!"

Connect with **Susan Ernst:** https://www.sueernst.com/

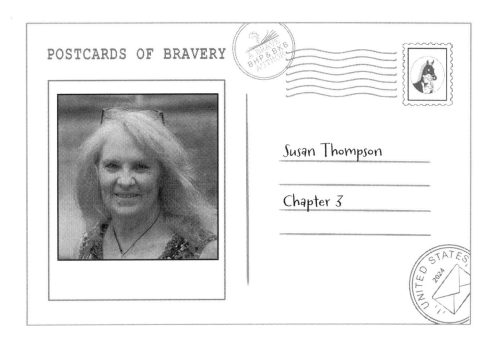

POSTCARDS OF BRAVERY

Susan Thompson

Chapter 3

Interested in horses and the welfare of all animals, she tells stories of rescuing the ones in need. Susan supports HeartstringsforHorses.com located in Granite Falls, Washington. Her proceeds from this story are donated to the rescue helping to save orphaned wild Mustang foals. Young horses are orphaned when 'Catchers' round up the adult horses in the wild and leave the young ones to fend for themselves. Many don't make it.

When the opportunity to collaborate with Brave Kids Books Publishing was offered, Susan knew she could get her voice out and bring awareness to this inhumane practice and help the world become a better place. Susan strives to spread kindness whenever possible.

Susan enjoys creative writing and bringing stories of bravery to our future world changers.

Connect with **Susan Thompson** at:
https://www.facebook.com/Littlebitty2

Janice Pratt

Chapter 4

I have dreamed of being an author since I was a young kid. I would write stories in my notebook, thinking that one day they would be a book. My first book, published at age 60, was long in the coming but not any less exciting. All those years of working in schools with amazing children have brought the Amaleigha stories to life. I learned throughout my teaching career that children can change the world but often just need a little support from those around them. I hope that Amaleigha inspires other children to make their dreams come true.

I am currently writing new Amaleigha stories and teaching online writing classes for children.

Connect with **Janice Pratt:** https://janpratt.com/

POSTCARDS OF BRAVERY

Samara Ena Minichiello

Chapter 5

Samara Ena Minichiello is a trauma-informed advocate for children globally. Her passion is to help children who cannot help themselves learn to be happy. She's a certified coach consultant with a trauma-informed certificate of completion and is a 'Happy for No Reason' certified trainer.

Samara spends her free time with family, friends, her miniature family poodle, Ally, or in her community volunteering. She has a weakness for dark chocolate, and her happy place is any pool with a picturesque, beautiful sun surrounded by palm trees.

For Samara, being part of *Brave Kids* Volume 1 and Volume 2 providing a channel to pass along wisdom to children who didn't know they have the power to 'choose' happy, is an honor. Before *Brave Kids,* Samara published her first Children's book in August 2022 called *The Secret: Magic of Your Heart,* which teaches young children how to unhurt their hurt hearts with agency.

Connect with **Samara Ena Minichiello** at:
https://thesecretmagicofyourheart.com

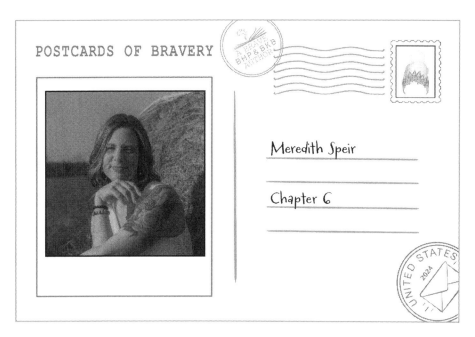

Meredith Speir

Chapter 6

Driven and inspired by her own personal life experiences, **Meredith Speir** is thrilled to publish her second short story with the help of *Brave Kids*. Meredith has a passion for empowering others to find purpose-filled lives. She is the co-founder and chief operating officer of The Recovery Connection in Winchester, Virginia. The Recovery Connection is a treatment provider for those who identify as female and struggle with substance use. Meredith is also a Registered Peer Recovery Specialist (RPRS) and has been in recovery from substance use disorder for over 14 years. She finds joy in working with those battling addiction, practicing yoga, shopping, and, most importantly, raising her beautiful daughter Caroline.

Connect with **Meredith Speir:** https://linktr.ee/meredith_speir23

POSTCARDS OF BRAVERY

Dr. Heidi MacAlpine

Chapter 7

Heidi MacAlpine is a mother of three adult children, podcaster, poet, writer, and an expert in working with children and adults with special needs and their families. Her personal and professional experience as a pediatric occupational therapist for 30+ years and a trauma-informed practitioner has assisted her in understanding the child and/or adult needs, strengths, interests, and barriers for a more holistic and safe perspective. Her programs are adapted and modified to work through overwhelming feelings and thoughts to overcome barriers, achieve goals, and improve relationships, and increase participation. She is a certified trauma practitioner, Trauma Informed Yoga Practitioner, and mindfulness educator. She has developed and implemented inclusive, fun, creative, and meaningful interventions and programs that address emotional, social, sensory, and physical needs using different mediums such as podcasts, storytelling, writing, animals, and nature exploration.

Connect with **Heidi MacAlpine** at: https://www.alignot.com/

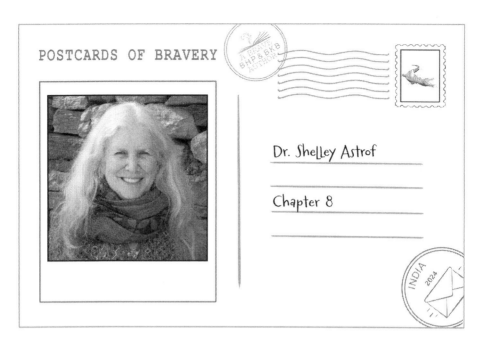

POSTCARDS OF BRAVERY

Dr. Shelley Astrof

Chapter 8

Shelley Astrof, a Peace Pioneer with a Doctor of Meditation degree and a passion for education (M.Ed.), brings the magic of over four decades spent in the company of a Great Teacher in the Himalayas.

She masterfully crafted *The Knower Curriculum,* an innovative holistic program seamlessly merging ancient wisdom with modern education—intertwining Meditation, Yoga, and Academics alongside *Timeless Tales*—enchanting young learners towards self-discovery.

Her empowering program equips children with invaluable tools for holistic well-being and lifelong success, fostering a generation of confident, empathetic individuals ready to embrace life's complexities with open hearts and resilient spirits.

Explore her vibrant "Knower Club"—an audio-video treasure trove where captivating stories and engaging Yoga practices await adventurous minds seeking to achieve their full potential.

Her classes in meditation and ancient scriptures take spiritual seekers beyond the Himalayan heights of awareness!

Are you ready to embark on this enchanting journey?
Connect with **Shelley Astrof** at: https://www.knower.ca/links

POSTCARDS OF BRAVERY

Dr. George Garcia, PhD, LMFT

Chapter 9

Dr. George Garcia, LMFT, Ph.D., is a licensed marriage and family therapist in the States of California and Ohio. He has worked in community outreach programs and private practices and has taught at the master's and doctoral levels.

His relentless passion for guiding others into greater healing and health is evident in the endeavors he's engaged in. Whether he is teaching graduate or doctoral students, training other therapists, or caring for his clients, George brings strong support and genuine commitment to helping others discover healing, health, and the best version of themselves.

When not in the office or classroom, you can find him being active in some capacity, whether it be rolling on the mats in a Jiu-Jitsu, attempting to hit a decent drive on the golf course, or chasing his young daughter and son around, he keeps active to stay healthy physically and mentally. He pursues learning through reading and maintains a close circle of friends.

Connect with **Dr. George Garcia** at: https://linktr.ee/drglmft

POSTCARDS OF BRAVERY

Kelly Daugherty, MSW, FT

Chapter 10

Kelly Daugherty, a seasoned social worker in Malta, New York, owns Greater Life Grief Counseling and the Center for Informed Grief, LLC. Her passion for grief support stems from her mother's death during her teenage years, inspiring her career.

Every day, Kelly finds meaning in her grief by helping individuals and professionals navigate the complexities of grief. She's a Fellow in Thanatology, specializing in death, dying, and bereavement.

Kelly has contributed her stories to the collaborative books *Holistic Mental Health: Calm, Clear and In Control for the Rest of Your Life*, Volume 1, *Brave Kids: Short Stories to Inspire Our Future World-Changers,* Volumes 1 and 2, and is the lead author in *The Grief Experience: Tools for Acceptance, Resilience, and Connection.*

Beyond work, she cherishes time with her husband, Kevin, and seven nieces and nephews. She enjoys DIY art projects, walking, running, and visiting Zoos, the beach, and Disney World.

Connect with **Kelly Daugherty:** https://linktr.ee/kellydaugherty

POSTCARDS OF BRAVERY

Indya J. Clark, LCSW

Chapter 11

Indya Clark has dedicated her life to helping others overcome adversity, trauma, and life detours as a licensed clinical social worker with 12 years of experience in handling trauma, PTSD, and life transitions. She is a trauma-informed resilience and mindset coach, anxiety and trauma therapist, and empowerment and transformation strategist.

Having received a full ride to the University of Denver, Indya received her master's in social work and a bachelor's degree in Sociology and Human Communications.

In December 2019, she founded Resilient Wings. As a mother of one older child and two young twins, Indya has both the educational background and the hands-on life experience to provide her with a deep understanding of the challenges that millennial and Gen Z mothers, as well as career women, face. This further inspired her to pursue a specialization in therapy, coaching, and training to help others grow and thrive despite what life might throw at them.

Connect with **Indya Clark:** https://www.resilientwings.com/

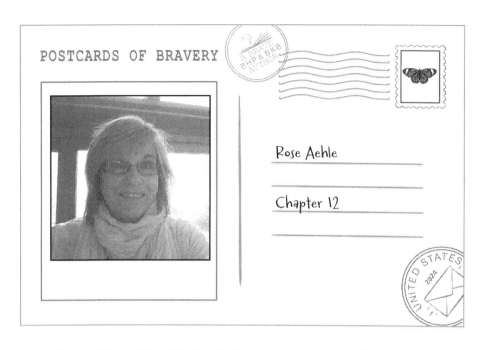

POSTCARDS OF BRAVERY

Rose Aehle

Chapter 12

Rose M Aehle, MS RT (R) (M), has been in the field of medical imaging for 44 years: 20 years as a radiographer (x-ray technologist) and 24 years as a program director/professor of a Radiologic Technology Program at Montgomery College in Takoma Park Maryland.

Outside of teaching, she has also always enjoyed writing short stories, which she did for her children when they were young. She crafted a picture book for young school-aged children about getting an X-ray titled *Nate Gets an X-ray*, which she has shared with children visiting the college.

She is honored with the opportunity to write a story that uses the fantasy of flying and the love of words, which was the inspiration behind "Superpowers." She believes we all have superpowers that can be used in brave and compassionate ways.

Connect with **Rose M Aehle** at:
https://www.facebook.com/profile.php?id=61553691763542

POSTCARDS OF BRAVERY

Lorie Weed

Chapter 13

Hi, my name is **Lorie Weed.** I'm a survivor. I work for a Fortune 500 company that contributes to saving many lives of our U.S. soldiers. At home, I spend my time practicing energy work to help people, animals, and nature heal. In my life, I am blessed to have a strong, bright, compassionate daughter who is my inspiration and her kind and thoughtful husband. Both of whom I appreciate dearly. My passion is protecting, caring for, and making way for the innocents of children and animals.

Connect with Lorie Weed: https://www.facebook.com/lorie.weed

POSTCARDS OF BRAVERY

Atlantis Wolf

Chapter 14

Atlantis Wolf is a professional shaman. That means she gets paid to invent ways to help people. She climbed corporate ladders in civil engineering and financial services until 2009, when her mom died. That moment awakened her spiritual gifts. She pivoted into healing arts, becoming an ordained shaman, master breathwork facilitator, and licensed medical massage therapist. Since 2010, she has helped over 3,000 clients manage or free themselves from chronic physical and emotional pain. Atlantis combines practical and intuitive modalities. Part of her secret is connecting to spiritual realms using breathwork, drumming, fire ceremonies, and guidance of galactic dragons. She leads breathwork events, writing courses, and group retreats. Sign up for her email list to receive a free video showing you how to release one piece of stuck energy with fire and drumming.

Connect with **Atlantis Wolf:** https://www.atlantiswolf.com/

Dr. Pamela J. Pine

Chapter 15

Dr. Pamela J. Pine has been a lifelong multimedia artist and is a best-selling author. She continues to enjoy a decade-long career in international health and child protection, particularly focused on enhancing the lives of underserved groups throughout the world.

"Amara" sprang forth from Pam's early and everlasting recognition and pondering of good and bad, right and wrong, kindness and cruelty, and magic that not only entertains but emboldens and sustains.

Some of the story of Amara and Her Mermaid sprung forth, too, from early memories. Pam remembers her ability to communicate through her favorite stuffed animals and a spirit world that supported her.

She continues to seek magic in her dealings with the world, knowing that creativity and wonder are what propels one forward and that life's magic is always there to find solutions to problems—one just needs to believe.

Connect with Dr. Pamela J. Pine at:
https://www.drpamelajpine.com

POSTCARDS OF BRAVERY

TJ STAR

Chapter 16

TJ STAR is a traveler, facilitator, creator, writer, and local guide based in Toronto (Tkaranto), Canada. She loves creating human-centered experiences for people to come together and connect with and explore all that is around them at home in Toronto and abroad. TJ has created the acronym S.T.A.R. (Start, Trust, Act, Risk Take) to empower others to live more intentionally and to spark their personal power. TJ or Thanuja as she is called, loves community engagement and supporting local businesses.

Connect with TJ STAR: https://linktr.ee/tj.thanuja

Dr. Charleen M. Michel

Chapter 17

Meet **Dr. Charleen M. Michel**

For nearly four decades, Charleen's been a scientist leading adventures in leadership development and diversity/inclusion. In 2016, she embarked on her spiritual journey, discovering secrets of the intellect, mind, and spirit to make life's choices sparkle with wisdom.

In 2023, she unveiled her sole-soulful venture, "Wisdom Unleashed with Charleen Michel – Paths to Self-Discovery." She's an enchantress in Ayurvedic Health, Chakra-Healing, Meditation, and Yoga, casting charms to help others listen to their inner whispers and orchestrate their life.

Charleen's passion as a hobby gardener connects her with nature's wisdom. It began during the summer holidays with her Grandpa. Now, he's her spirit guide as she creates enchanting English Rose and Alpine Gardens. Her essence is "Rose Goldea"—a fragrance inspired by her garden experiences.

Journey into magical realms and discover spiritual paths to unleash your inner wisdom.

Connect with **Dr. Charleen M. Michel** at:
https://www.wisdomunleashed.ch/

MJ Luna, OTR/L

Chapter 18

MJ Luna is an occupational therapist who worked many years in healthcare and the public school system before opening her own practice specializing in myofascial release. MJ is passionate about guiding her clients on their healing journey. She takes a holistic approach, and not only does she assist them in releasing pain from their bodies, but she also brings awareness to their mental constructs. It's rewarding to see people return to a pain-free life both physically and emotionally and transform into the best version of themselves through conscious awareness.

MJ is enrolled in an herbalism program and plans on adding this approach to her practice upon completion in 2025.

She has a special interest in educating our youth, preserving our natural environments, and providing resources to hunger and abuse victims.

MJ is a nature enthusiast and loves the great outdoors! She spends her time hiking, camping, climbing mountains, biking, swimming, stand-up paddleboarding, downhill skiing, observing animals, identifying plants/ trees, and appreciating the beauty of nature. She also loves adventuring, especially to foreign countries, and continues her quest to travel worldwide.

Connect with **MJ Luna** at: https://www.sunstarhealingmfr.com

Terri Hawke

Chapter 19

Terri Hawke is a naturalist, writer, animal communicator, energy healer, environmental educator, and retired environmental planner. She makes her home in Port Townsend, Washington. She has spent much of her life observing nature and immersing herself in different ecosystems all over the United States.

She is an animal guardian to dogs, Templeton and Trixie, and her cat, Maura. When not writing, she is laughing at her dog's wrestling, chasing her cat, reading, watching classic kids' cartoons, or out in nature finding healing.

After losing her adult son, Allen, and realizing that most people do not know how to deal with the emotional upheaval of grief, she decided to use her writing skills to help children so they can grow up to be happier adults healthily processing grief. Much of the process includes connecting to the wonders of the natural world.

Connect with **Terri Hawke:**
https://www.facebook.com/profile.php?id=61553824022128

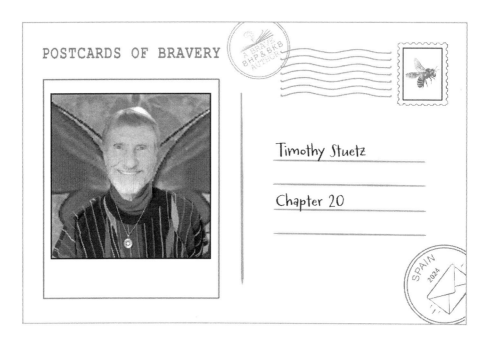

Timothy Stuetz

Chapter 20

Timothy Stuetz, The Magical Fairy Tale Creator

Welcome to my fantastical, inspirational, educational world of fairy tales, enhancing children's brain development, creativity, social skills, self-esteem, and OVERALL BRILLIANCE.

Creatively weaving myth/mystery, fantasy/reality, poetry, and proven principles of child development, I've authored more fairy tales (160+) than the legendary Hans Christian Andersen. Sparkling, bountiful blessings for ALL!

Chockfull of heroes, heroines, and captivating characters like Bliss Beary Bear, Poet Bear, Beeleev'n Bear, Beddy-Bye Bear, and Power Animal Pals, they anchor a unique book club featuring live story times, parent support circles, and more—every month.

A master of multiple ancient arts-sacred sciences, my Yoda Youth Instructor Program empowers and certifies teens to teach multiple holistic health and complementary medical modalities globally by age 18.

A certified children's coach, ordained minister, retired CPA, and dad with 72 years of life experience, I serve and spark people to live their full potential with God's grace, radiant love, and soulful bliss.

Connect with **Timothy Stuetz** at: https://linktr.ee/timothystuetz.com

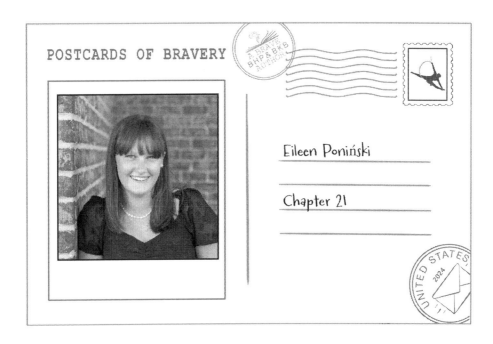

POSTCARDS OF BRAVERY

Eileen Poniński

Chapter 21

Eileen Poniński, a dynamic high school junior, enchants audiences with her trombone in the marching band while nurturing dreams of studying architectural design and restoration. As a dedicated Girl Scout Ambassador for over a decade, Eileen is on a mission to earn her Gold Award, showcasing her commitment to community impact.

Beyond her academic pursuits, Eileen is a captivating aerial artist, effortlessly defying gravity, and a self-taught contortionist, pushing the boundaries of physical artistry. Her diverse talents reflect a passionate spirit ready to leave an indelible mark on the world.

Eileen Poniński is not merely a Texas student but a symphony of creativity, resilience, and ambition, poised to shape a future that extends far beyond the ordinary.

Connect with **Eileen Poniński** at: https://msha.ke/eileen.life

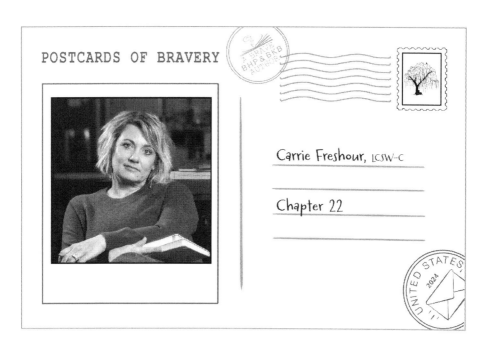

POSTCARDS OF BRAVERY

Carrie Freshour, LCSW-C

Chapter 22

Carrie Freshour, the force behind Carrie Freshour Consulting, leverages 25+ years as a seasoned licensed clinical social worker. Her firm serves as a catalyst for empowering individuals and teams, fostering resilience, and breaking down the stigma embedded in workplace culture. As an author, consultant, and motivational speaker, Carrie fearlessly guides transformative conversations, initiating breakthroughs in challenging situations.

In executive leadership, she shapes programs, policies, and curricula across diverse settings. With a background weaving lived experience, clinical acumen, and executive leadership, Carrie leads with unwavering purpose and inspiring breakthroughs.

She enjoys spending time with her husband and two children, writing, cooking, playing soccer, and exploring cultures.

Her journey manifests a commitment to inclusive cultures and transformative change. Rooted in empathy and accountability, she pioneers a path where stigma shatters, bravery thrives, and every child finds their voice against abuse.

Connect with **Carrie Freshour** at:
https://www.carriefreshourconsulting.com/

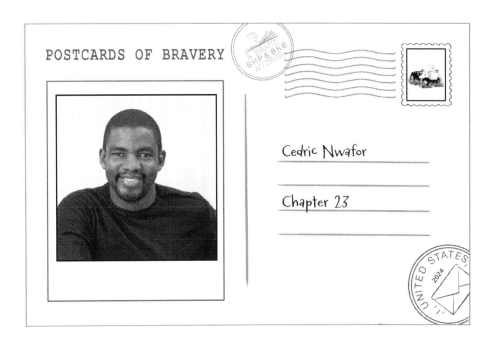

Cedric Nwafor

Chapter 23

A passion for agriculture and its people drives **Cedric Nwafor.** He believes engaging younger generations in agriculture is vital to the African continent's future and its people's socio-economic well-being. Cedric co-founded and serves as the Executive Director of Roots Africa.

After graduating from the University of Maryland College of Agriculture, he continued his affiliation with the college. He developed the Innovation and Entrepreneurship Program, developed a course on Global Agriculture, and received a Graduate Certificate in Non-Profit Management from the School of Public Policy.

Cedric is also a member of the Board of Directors of the Center for Technology Access and Training (CETAT). He received an award for Most Innovative Project from Universitas 21 and won the Do Good Challenge from UMD.

Leadership Idaho Agriculture has recognized his work by naming him an Honorary Lifetime Affiliate Member, and the University of Maryland Alumni Association named him the 2022 Outstanding Young Alumnus Award winner at the Maryland.

Connect with **Cedric Nwafor:** https://www.linkedin.com/in/cedricnwafor/

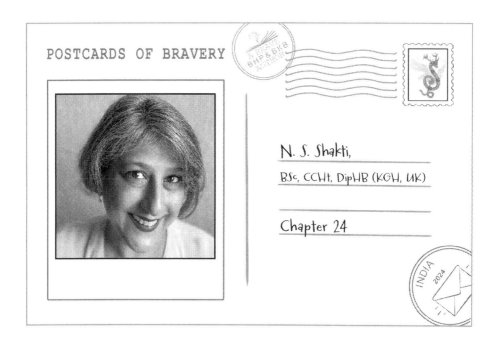

N. S. Shakti,

BSc, CCHt, DipHB (KGH, UK)

Chapter 24

N.S. Shakti, or **Natasha Sharma** as she is known when she is not authoring, was born in England and now lives in India. She has traveled the world and has tons of certificates. She has learned some amazing things both about herself and the universe. She loves teaching people through her experiences of life.

She does this best by speaking and writing about them in internationally bestselling books. This is her 5th book and her 2nd children's book.

Natasha means resurrection, so it's no surprise that her spirit animal is the snake, which holds divine, ancient, powerful feminine energy.

She embodies the healing powers of the self, birth, death, rebirth, transformation, self-realization, radical acceptance, and choice.

Stepping into the raw power of Shakti—of the life force, kundalini energy, and the ability to see and activate is her divine gift and purpose in the world.

Connect with **N.S. Shakti:**
https://www.linktr.ee/natashasharma.shakti

Acknowledgments

*S*tar light, star bright, the first star I see tonight. I wish I may, I wish I might, have this wish I wish tonight. . .

These dear words I whispered as I looked up towards the first star.

Thank you, dear star light, star bright, the first star I saw upon many nights. Thank you for all my wishes I made upon many nights as I gazed upon your fare, sparkling sight.

Thank you Mom and Dad for your guidance and belief in your daughters. Thank you Sis for your constant companionship and for being my *best'est* of friends. Thank you Oupa for being my rock, and thank you Fred for taking his place. Thank you Laura Di Franco for your wisdom and partnership, and thank you, my dearest *Brave Kids, Vol. 2* authors, for your strength, your determination, belief in me, and your rewrites, and a special thank you to Shelley Astrof, who helped me with mine.

And lastly, thank you to Child White Dragon's sisters and their authors, Atlantis Wolf, for sharing Emmy with us, and N.S. Shakti, also known as Natasha Sharma, for giving me the gift of Namati's metamorphosis and my own transformation.

Dear reader, dear passenger of this HMS Explorer, thank you for your bravery and for embracing you. You are special. You are brilliant. And your life and your living it has a purpose beyond your wildest of dreams.

be brave dear Child
By K.J. Kaschula

be brave dear Child,
not because you have to
or because you must.
be brave for your heart
and for your soul,
be brave for the stillness of your mind,
and the chaos roaming from within.
know that a light shines,
a bright light,
a brave light,
your truth light.

Embrace the coming darkness,
the lesson needed to be learned,
the hardship needed to be endured,
the journey needed to be traveled.
for only the coming darkness
can welcome the light.

ignight this light,
dear Child.
your truth light,
your brave light,
your bright light.
let it shine
let it burn.
let it fuel your mind,
your soul,
and your heart.
so, be brave dear Child.

Books by K.J. Kaschula
The-Super-Dooper-Secret-Collection:
I Caught One of Santa's Reindeer
I Captured the Easter Bunny's Chicken

Brave Kids: Short Stories
to Inspire Future World-Changers
Volumes 1 & 2

For more information about the above titles
write or visit the author's website at:

www.kjkaschula.com